ON THE VERGE OF EXTINCTION

A science-fiction novel

by

Migul. I. Shyamalen

MIGUL ILAVARASU SHYAMALEN

PART 1

Many, many years ago

Year: 2019

CHAPTER 1: INTRODUCTION

It was a black Rolls-Royce Cullinan. It rolled into the Liberty Space Research Organization (LSRO) parking lot majestically. A young and energetic man stepped out. No one bothered him for identity cards or anything of that sort while he entered past the gate into the building.

Everyone knew who he was. Security around the building was tight. This was one of the most successful space research organizations that are being dealt with over here. Extreme precautions had been taken.

There were multiple watchtowers all over. The surrounding walls were five feet thick and had electric fencing running all around. The electric fences were no joke. If anybody ever touched it, they would instantly be incinerated. There were armed men all over. Every man carried a semi-automatic pistol and an AK-47. They were all wearing camo and probably had somebody armor too. The entire base was built on acres and acres of land. It had three hundred and eighty acres of land to be precise. It had all the space to research, plan, build and launch just about anything. There was a huge launch pad at the heart of the whole land. There was also a secondary launch pad if in case there was a problem with the primary launch pad and something had to be launched immediately. Every aspect was meticulously planned. There were multiple hangars and construction sites. The man who got down from the car went straight to the largest building over there. He went in through the doors briefly scanning his ID card against the electric card reader. A green light glowed once he scanned his card. If he was not an authorized person, the card reader would have set off multiple alarms all around the building. The person entering would have been surrounded by at least 10 men with guns in less than 7 seconds. The man entered the building. The building looked like it did not even belong in 2019. The building was so advanced and heavily furnished. For starters, the carpet was made from very high-quality material and was several inches thick. Any normal person would never walk on that carpet with shoes on. The man was in a long corridor with the front desk in the far end. There were expensive leather sofas all along both sides of the corridor as this was the waiting area. The wall was designed beautifully too. There were many paintings hung up on the wall, all based on space and space research. The man walked confidently towards the front desk. He was wearing an expensive black suit with a peach shirt and a red tie. The tie was bright and shiny. He was wearing a pair of Ray-Ban sunglasses, but he left them behind in the car. Most importantly he had a smile on his face. He reached the front desk.

A lady was wearing a white shirt and a red skirt. She was sitting behind the front desk. Somehow her clothes suited her job.

"Hello sir, how may I help you?" She asked. Her name was Lucy. Lucy Warner. She was the newest staff member and the only person in LSRO to not know the man standing on the other side of the front desk.

"Hi, may I know where Mr. Jake Camber is?"

The man replied. "May I know the reason for

meeting him?" Lucy asked.

"Oh, I just have to hand over this file

to him." The man said. "Can I see your

visitor's permit?" Lucy asked.

"I don't have a visitor's permit. I work over here. I just have to give this file to him, and I can go to my office." The man said.

"Show me your identity card please" Lucy requested.

He was reaching for his identity card when

he heard a voice. "Lucy, what in the world are

you doing?!" The voice shrieked.

The man turned. The voice came from a short man with his hair completely shaved off. He had a heavy American accent but his skin tone would suggest he was from some middle African country. It was Jake Camber. He was staring dead at Lucy. Lucy now was almost crying.

"I'm sorry sir....I... I don't understand what is happening." She stammered.

"Do you know who this man is?!" He boomed.

"Jake, I suggest you calm down," The man said. "She's new here.   She is just doing her job". He turned to Lucy. "I am very happy that you are doing your job very well. Keep it up". He said.

"Thank you, sir,", said Lucy.

The man and Jake left, heading towards the elevator to the left of the front desk, the same elevator Jake had come down in.

Jake's anger towards Lucy was indeed justifiable. The man who had just spoken to Lucy was a very important person for LSRO. His name was Mike Hensworth. He was in charge of the plan, construction and launch of every single spacecraft form LSRO. He was an incredibly talented man. He could fix just about any problem that arises and think of solutions that nobody would have ever dreamt of. Most of the rockets that were launch until now could have never been possible without Mike Hensworth.

They had reached the 24ᵗʰ floor of the 55-story building. They went through the corridor and entered a room at the end of it. They were now in a large but empty room. There was an oak table at one corner of the room next to a window that looked over the secondary launch pad. The whole room was carpeted. The walls had wallpapers that looked like wood. There was one large leather chair behind the table and two smaller leather chairs in front of the table. There also was a large fireplace. Although it wasn't used in a very long time, it still added a luxurious touch to the room.

"Are you done looking through the file Mr. Hensworth?" asked Jake.

"Yes Jake, I went through the entire plan and the plan looks to be solid. I think if the CEO goes through the plan once, we can immediately start construction." Mike said. "I'll just leave the file on your table Jake."

"Sure Mr. Mike, thank you so much for your time", Jake said as he was fiddling with the AC remote trying to get it to work. Mike Hensworth left without saying anything else.

He went over to the elevator and pressed the up arrow. Mike's office was located on the 55th floor. There were only two rooms on that floor; one that was the office of Mike Hensworth and the other which was the office of the CEO of LSRO.

Once the elevator opened on the 24th floor, Mike hit the button marked 55. The button also read Mike's fingerprint as he pressed the button. Again, if he wasn't authorized, he would have set off a bunch of alarms. After about a minute, he reached the highest floor of the building. He stepped out of the elevator and went over to the door of his office. He could not just stick a key in the keyhole and enter the room. As a matter of fact, there was no keyhole. There was an array of security measures but a mere lock and key weren't one of them. First, he had to scan the entire surface of his right and left palm on the laser palm print reader. Once that is done, there will be a retina scan. Both the retinas will be scanned. Finally, there will be a 16 digit code. If there happened to be an error in any of the scanning process, a second chance would be given. If the second time also ends up in an error, there would be a couple of guards at the door the very next instant.

Mike finished all the security checks and got in. Mike's room was bigger and better than in Jake's room. There was a bigger oak table next to a bigger window but this window looked over the main launchpad and not the secondary launch pad. There also was a bigger fireplace. This one looked like it was used more recently. There were multiple AC vents and one centralized air conditioning system. There were five ceilings to floor paintings that covered about 70 percent of the wall area. The rest of the wall surface was covered with inexpensive wallpaper.

There was a very nice and expensive carpet on the floor, maroon and several inches thick. There was a huge TV screen. There were six single seater sofas, all of them made with alligator leather. Not to mention their massage function. They were also heated and ventilated. Mike's desk setup was similar to Jake's.

Mike closed the room door behind him and walked over to his seat behind his desk. He went over and sat there. He was thinking about the file that he read.

The file contained all the information about LSRO's latest and most expensive space mission yet. He remembered the name written on the file-

JETLAX 4000

The prototype was made a few weeks ago. Mike looked at that too. He approved the design. Now only the CEO has to take a look at the file and the construction shall begin. Sitting at his desk he briefly smiled. As usual, he was in charge of the whole thing.

CHAPTER 2: THE VAULT

It was now a few days later. The CEO of LSRO, Mr. Brandon Lync, had gone through both the file and the prototype and had approved the project. Today was the day mission JETLAX 4000 was scheduled to start. Everything was going according to plan. Obviously, nothing could ever begin without Brandon Lync and Mike Hensworth.

Mike was lying cross-legged on his bed when his alarm went off. He quickly shut the alarm off and from a sleeping position on his bed, he went to a sitting position on his bed. He sat there thinking about the big day that he was about to live. Mission JETLAX 4000 had an investment worth about 97 percent of the company's worth. This was the largest investment the CEO of LSRO has ever made and the biggest risk he has ever taken. Any sort of error or mistake was too great to afford. There just cannot be any mistakes. And the scariest part of all was the fact that Mike was the person in charge of the whole thing. If this mission is successful, it would earn 230 percent of the original investment.

Mike got up from the bed and went into his bathroom. His bathroom was big, very big. Mike lived in a mansion that had 6 bedrooms and was 4 stories high. Mike was not married although he did have a girlfriend. They were going to get married in one of the first few months of 2020.

Mike's girlfriend's name was Sarah. Sarah Billingwood. Sarah stays with Mike for most of the days but just three days ago she had gone to meet her parents so Mike was staying alone. Mike had no parents. Both his parents had passed away in an extreme accident. They died in a plane crash. They were both flying to the Maldives for a vacation while they left Mike back at home. This happened just a few months ago.

Mike went to the airport to send them off. His parents were scheduled to return in just eight days. Mike had no clue that his parents would never return nor did he know that this would be the last time he was seeing his parents. He wanted to leave immediately but he for some reason decided to stay until his parent's flight takes off. His parents were traveling first class, and the thought of his parents having that luxury made Mike smile. But that smile did not last for long. Soon the plane took off. A few seconds into the flight, as soon as it crossed the airport border all four of the Airbus A380's engines simultaneously exploded, sending the whole plane in a nose dive straight into the concrete pavement killing 7 civilians on the pavement and about 80 percent of the passengers inside the plane. Sadly, Mike's parents were two of the 80 percent of passengers who died. A few days after the plane crash, the investigation team said there was fuel leakage in all of the engines and when the temperature of the engines crossed ignition temperature, they exploded. That was the end of that.

After about 45 minutes, Mike was done bathing. He liked bathing a lot. He would just lay in the bathtub and think of what he had done or what he was about to do. Right now his mind was completely on what lay ahead. He was out of the bathroom and went into his closet. He planned on wearing an all-black suit and pants, with a light blue shirt and a gold and bronze striped tie. It was an antique. He went down to the ground floor, to the kitchen, straight to the espresso machine. Mike loved coffee. His coffee was steaming hot and ready for him to drink. He drank his coffee and made himself a simple chicken sandwich along with a fruit salad and a pancake. He also made himself a chocolate protein milkshake. He preferred to cook on his own rather than to have someone cook the food for him.

Once he was done eating, he went on and wore his shoes. He wore a pair of black formal Gucci. He was all set for his big day. He checked himself in the ceiling to floor mirror one last time and headed out the door. He headed to his garage. Just like his house, the garage was massive. He had many antique and exotic cars. He had a Rolls-Royce that was his daily driver. It was a Cullinan and it was heavily customized. Mike was extremely wealthy but he did not like showing off his wealth. The Cullinan wasn't the only car he had. He had a Mercedes-Benz Maybach limousine, a Lamborghini Aventador, a Bugatti Chiron and last but not least an extremely old, vintage car.

He picked his Cullinan. He got in and drove straight to the LSRO headquarters.

He entered in, drove to the parking lot, parked his car there and went into his office. The construction was officially supposed to start at 9 am. When Mike reached his office, it was just 7:30 am.

He was sitting at his desk, thinking about his parents. He was almost tearing when his intercom buzzed. It was Brandon Lync.

"Mr. Mike Hensworth, can you please come to my office?" Brandon asked. "Sure sir, what's the matter. Is everything alright?" asked Mike.

"Come to my office, I'll tell you

everything."

"Sure sir, I'm on my way."

Brandon Lync's office was as good as Mike Hensworth's office. Everything looked almost identical except one thing. There was a large, dome-shaped metal door that covered almost one entire wall. It was silver in color and had something on it that looked like a ship's steering wheel. This was the first time Mike had ever seen his CEO's room.

"Mr. Mike Hensworth", he began. "As you already know, you are working in the world's most successful private space organization. LSRO has been through a lot of problems and you were always the one to fix them. You might as well know that our rocket software and technology is more advanced than any other company in the world. That might be one of the reasons why we are so successful. But there is one more thing that is more important than any of the software; the Heart Analytic Space Research Engine and Transmitter or HASRET in short."

"Ok sir, but what makes you call me here?" asked Mike.

"I'm coming to that Mr. Mike", Brandon continued. "As you know I would have never called you personally if it hadn't been so important. This vault you see behind me is the heart of LSRO. This is where we keep the HASRET."

Mike turned to the vault. He kept staring at it. It stood there, big and bold. As mike was staring at the vault, Brandon walked over to the vault. There was a metal plate next to the big dome. He went over and put his right palm over the metal plate. Suddenly there was a red laser scanning his palm. The next moment the metal plate disappeared into the wall and the screen popped out. Next to the screen a cube also seemed to appear from nowhere. The cube had a glass surface only on the top, the rest was pure steel. The screen had the numbers from 1 to 9, arranged in the form of a keypad. Brandon typed in a sixteen-digit number on the screen. The screen then flashed green. Then a little camera popped up from the top of the screen. He leaned forward. He first got his right eye in front of the camera and then his left eye. After both, his eyes were scanned he then put his right palm on the glass cube. The glass cube flashed green. Then it did the same when he put his left palm on the screen. Then finally a little microphone popped up instead of the camera that scanned his eye. He leaned towards the microphone and said 'Matrix Open'. Then there was a heavy sounding metal click.

Brandon then started spinning the wheel on the dome in the anti- clockwise direction.

As he was spinning the wheel, he turned to Mike.

"Mr. Mike", he began. "There is a reason behind me showing you all this. I know today is the day that we are going to start the construction of JETLAX 4000 and since it is our most expensive project, I could not help but show the HASRET of JETLAX 4000 to you. Also, I thought it was important for you to know this as you are the director of JETLAX 4000. Taking a look at this and its modifications might want you to tweak a few things in the design to make it faster, more powerful and more efficient."

Just as he finished his sentence, there was another click from the vault. The vault was now open.

Brandon reached out to the handle and slightly pulled on the handle. Then he retreated back. There was some motor that kicked in because there was a slight whirring noise from the vault. The vault's door was motorized. This was mainly for one reason; the door weight just too much to be pulled by hand. The door took about thirty seconds to open. Once the vault opened, there was a fan automatically turned on to clear a white mist.

And then there it was.

The HASRET was placed on a white platform. The HASRET was a perfect cube. It was radiating a bright blue color. It has a beautiful mess of printed circuit boards inside. It truly looked like a work of art.

"Mr. Mike Hensworth, I give you the HASRET of the JETLAX 400", said Brandon.

Mike was speechless. He was totally lost for words. He has seen many HASRETs before but none as big, beautiful and elegant as this. Mike knew that most of the money involved in mission JETLAX 4000 was to create the beast in front of him.

"This will be added to the rocket as you said at the 5th phase of the construction of the rocket right Mr. Mike?" asked Brandon.

"Yes sir", replied Mike confidently with his eyes still fixed on the HASRET. His eyes were gleaming. "Can I close it Mr. Mike?" asked Brandon after he saw that Mike's eyes were drilling into the HASRET.

"Uh…oh yes, sir sure. I'm sorry if I took too much of your time", said Mike. "Oh it's absolutely fine", said Brandon as he was closing the vault.

The vault was closed and locked by Brandon. Locking the vault was much simpler than opening it. Brandon pressed a button next to the vault. As soon as he pressed the button, the vault whirred closed. Then Brandon spun the wheel in the clockwise direction until it spun no more. Then, he turned to the screen. There was a red circle on the screen that read 'LOCK'. Brandon touched the red button on the screen. Then there was the same click sound and the screen, the microphone, and the steel cube disappeared and the metal plate appeared back.

Mike watched all of this silently. After Brandon locked the vault, he walked over to Mike.

"Oh look it is 8:55", said Brandon. "Jake should be here any minute to take us for the launch and the press meet."

Sure enough in about a minute, Jake Camber was there to take Brandon and Mike down to the press meet and launch. As soon as he called Brandon and Mike were ready and headed out the door to begin their all- new adventure with JETLAX 4000.

Neither Mike nor Brandon had noticed the small penny-sized microphone attached to Mike's shoe and neither of them was aware that the entire conversation that just took place was heard by the person who attached it.

CHAPTER 3: BEGINNING AND THE END

All three of them went down together in the elevator. None of them spoke during the elevator ride. Brandon briefly looked at his watch and Mike coughed a little bit. After about two minutes, they reached the ground floor. Jake was the first one to come out followed by Brandon and Mike. All three of them walked over to Lucy who was ready to take them to the press meet.

The press meet was held first. Brandon Lync was to clear a few doubts about the mission that the reporters and the public had and then it was time for the launch. This is how Brandon liked it. He liked press meet first and then the launch. This stops the reporters from asking too many unnecessary questions about the project.

Brandon attended the press meet, everything went normally. Then it was time for the launch.

Brandon being the CEO of LSRO, hosted most of the launch. Then Mike was sent to give a few words on this and he was done in a jiffy. The stage in itself was massive. It looked so seamless and the entire presentation was carried out effortlessly. Brandon told the public about their main intension with JETLAX 4000.   JETLAX 4000 was mainly designed to help the world get a better understanding of our solar system. It was designed in such a way that it would visit Mars, Jupiter, Saturn and Neptune and collect crucial information about each of these different planets. This information will then be used to develop technology for future space living. There is even a chance that JETLAX 4000 will bring back a few samples to run tests on but that was not a guarantee. The stage was incredible. There was a huge seamless curved screen running the entire back wall and extending through the sides too.

The screen was also extremely high-resolution 8k so the entire project looked that much more interesting.

After the presentation was over Brandon and Mike went back to their respective offices to get their files and the construction was to start at 1 pm that afternoon after the engineers and other related people eat some lunch and get a bit of rest after that tiring presentation.

It was just 12 pm then and Mike decided to eat in a nearby restaurant as it had been a long time since he ate outside and he wanted a change.

He had a simple lunch; a barbeque chicken rice bowl and an orange juice. Then he returned. He was just in time. After about ten minutes post Mike's arrival at LSRO, the construction began.

The work was done vigorously that day. They finally finished that day's work at about 11 pm. Mike could have stayed at the LSRO headquarters as there was a nice bedroom for him and most of the other engineers at LSRO but Mike decided to head home. He reached home in about twenty minutes as there was no traffic and the Cullinan's engine just made things easier and smoother for Mike. He drove up to his garage and parked his car inside. He got out of the car and went inside his house. He was untying his shoelace when he noticed the penny-sized burn hole in his left shoe. That was extremely strange to him. That was very random. He had no idea that the hole was from the microphone self-destructing after it overheard the conversation.

He was very, very tired after the long day. Without even changing into some nightclothes, he went to the kitchen and made himself some dinner. He ate a piece of grilled steak and mashed potatoes for dinner. Then he went to his bathroom upstairs and had a nice shower. He used the shower and not the bathtub. After he was done he went to his basement gym and did a quick thirty-minute workout. Then he went into the living room and watched about half a movie before he dozed off on the recliner.

This was how Mike liked to spend the night before

the day he had no work. His CEO had given him a day off without even Mike asking for it. He knew that Mike would be tired after the presentation.

The next morning he woke up pretty late at about 8:30 am. He went through his normal routine; he brushed, bathed and ate. He wanted to watch some television but just could not. There was something constantly going through his head; HOW DID THAT HOLE ON HIS SHOE APPEAR?!?!?!

He somehow got it off his mind and watched some TV. The day slowly passed and ended as usual.

The next day he went to work and things went on as usual. As usual, whenever a problem occurred, Mike was the one to fix it. There were countless problems that he fixed all the way from electrical to hardware problems.

A few months passed and it was New Year's Eve. This was a very special day for Mike Hensworth. Today, in about a few hours he was going to meet Sarah after many months. Sarah was to call once she lands and Mike was to go and pick her up. It was around 9 pm; Sarah was scheduled to land at 11:10 pm. As usual, Mike was at home watching Stranger Things on Netflix. Mike liked to binge-watch. He did it every night on every holiday. A few episodes later, he got up to go to the airport to pick her up. He wore a pair of brown sandals and went over to his garage. He had the Lamborghini key in hand. The Aventador was Sarah's favorite car and it was no surprise that Mike chose to pick her up with it. The airport wasn't very far away. Although there was a good amount of traffic, Mike drove to the airport in about 45 minutes. 45 minutes was actually relatively quick. There had been times that Mike was stuck in traffic for well over two hours.

He was waiting for about 15 minutes. Then Sarah came out of the airport. She briefly searched for the car but the Aventador stood out like a sword. She went over to the car and looked in. As she was looking in, Mike came out of nowhere and scared the life out of Sarah. Sarah shouted so loudly that half the people around were staring at her.

"Mike what are you doing?!" beamed Sarah. "Happy new year's eve", said Mike. "Wow, some welcome", said Sarah. "Come on get in let's go", she added.

Sarah was about to get into the passenger's seat when Mike stopped her.

"You drive", he said. "Are you sure Mike because the last time I drove the Lamborghini, you almost puked of nausea", she said.

"Yes, I'm sure", he added. Without any further discussion, Sarah grabbed the keys from Mike's hand and got into the driver's seat. Mike got into the passenger's seat.

Mike was indeed scared. Sarah was an extremely fast driver. Although Sarah knows what she is doing, Mike still freaks out when she drives.
On a moderately empty freeway, she could easily drive at about 106 miles per hour. Mike would be thrown out of his comfort zone at those speeds.

Sarah thankfully wasn't in the mood of driving that fast today. But that did not mean she drove slow in any means. She was driving at an average of around 90 miles per hour. On the way back there was very little or no traffic. She got them both home in no more than 25 minutes.
Sarah was very tired after she reached home. She had flown a long flight. She, unlike usual, had just flown premium economy whereas she usually prefers business class or first class. This time she was a little late to book and she had no seats available in either of those two classes.

Mike was also tired but both of them decided to stay awake till New Year.

And they did. They were awake till New Year and at around 1:30 pm, both of them went to bed. Both of them were so tired that they literally passed out.

The next morning was as usual when both of them were together. Mike had purposefully switched his alarm off because he wanted to sleep in late. Unfortunately, Sarah woke him up with a cup of steaming hot cappuccino. Sarah had already bathed and also cooked breakfast. She had prepared some bacon strips and a burrito for breakfast. Mike quickly woke up, brushed his teeth, drank his coffee and went down for breakfast. Sarah and Mike ate together watched Stanger Things on Netflix Literally all day long. Stranger Things was the only show that both of them like. Every other show on Netflix is always a 'Mike like' 'Sarah' hate situation or 'Sarah like' 'Mike hate' situation.

They were so into watching the show that they forgot to eat lunch and they directly ate dinner. The next day both of them had work. Sarah owned a chain of spas called 'RELAX THERAPY'.

Many days passed and JETLAX 4000 was nearing completion. Everything was constructed, checked and double-checked for any errors or flaws. Everything was in working order and supreme condition.

Mike was in his office going through a few project details when he got a call from his CEO, Brandon Lync.
"Mr. Mike, can you please come over to my office for a second please?" he asked. "Yes sir, sure. I'm coming right now", said Mike.

Brandon's office was exactly how he remembered it. There was absolutely no change. Even the temperature felt the same.

"Mr. Mike tomorrow is the big day", he said. "The HASRET is going to go into the rocket tomorrow.

Tomorrow is the day we are going to completely finish the construction of JETLAX 4000. This is such a crucial part of the project. If we somehow fail tomorrow the entire project is a failure and that sort of a loss can be compensated only by selling this entire company."

"I understand sir. There will be no such failure tomorrow. I can assure you that." said Mike.

"Very well then Mike, if you want you can go home now and come back tomorrow no later than 9 am. I am planning on installing the HASRET at 10:30 am", said Brandon.

"Sure sir, I will be back tomorrow at 9 am", said Mike. "Ok then, have a good day", said the CEO.

"You too have a good day sir!", said Mike as he was leaving the office. Mike went home, showered and then went to bed.

He woke up pretty early the next morning. He went through his normal routine and got ready for the big day. The HASRET was to be installed into JETLAX 4000 that day. Mike was nervous yet excited. This was the day JETLAX 4000 would officially be complete. If today went all ok then JETLAX 4000 would be in space in a couple of weeks.

It was 8:30 am and Mike was already on his way to the LSRO headquarters. There was a lot of traffic. Soon he eventually reached his office. He went through the installation booklet that Lucy had given him on his way to the office. There was something odd. Brandon had strongly insisted Mike be on time but Brandon himself was not at the LSRO headquarters at that moment. This felt very unusual to Mike.

Brandon was always on time if not early. Mike had initially thought that it could be some traffic but it was more than half an hour since the usual arriving time of Brandon.

Mike was sitting in his chair moving uncomfortably when he heard a knock on his door. "Come in", he shouted. The door opened and a young woman with blonde hair walked in.

There was something about the way she walked. She walked confidently but it did not seem aggressive. There are very few people in the world who can both be confident but at the same time not arrogant.

Although her face gave nothing away Mike guessed that the upcoming news may not be very good.

"Good morning sir", she said. "My name is Katie Broster. I am CEO Brandon Lync's personal assistant. I am here to inform you about the delivery to you just a few minutes ago. We could have gotten it to you over here but it is a large duffel bag and it is quite heavy. It is placed near the secondary launch pad."

"Sure I'll take a look at it", said Mike. "Sure sir, have a

nice day", said Katie and left.

In about 5 minutes Mike got up and left. He headed to the secondary launch pad. And there it was a large, black duffel bag with a white zipper. There were about 15 people watching him as he opened it.

It struck him hard as soon as he opened the bag. It felt as if a 10 ton boulder had just fallen on him. He was immediately thrown back. He could not believe his eyes. A couple of people who were watching him open the bag ran towards the bag and had a look inside. Everyone was speechless. Mike absolutely did not believe his eyes. He took another look and only then confirmed that this was real and not some sort of bad dream. It was Brandon Lync inside the bag. He was dead and covered in blood. There was something more horrific. Both his eyes were missing and both his hands were cut off at the elbow.

That was when it struck Mike. He had used only his eyes and hands as physical parts of his body to unlock the vault in which the HASRET was stored. Mike feared the worst. He immediately got to his feet and ran towards the main building. He went straight into the lift and hit the button that read 55. After about two minutes he reached the 55th floor. He ran to Brandon's door. Sure enough, the only security measure before entering was the retina scan and Brandon had neither of his two retinas attached to his face at the moment. Soon a bunch of staff and engineers arrived on the 55th floor. It looked like Katie already knew the problem that Mike would face because she made one of the engineers to get a laser cutter. The engineer immediately got to work. He cut down the hinges in less than three minutes and the door finally fell open. It set off a bunch of alarms but no one cared.

No one could believe what they saw. The vault was wide open. Next to the vault laid Brandon's eyes and hands. It was a truly horrific scene.
But that was not the worst what they saw. Mike turned his head and saw something the devastated him. It was the HASRET. It was crushed into a zillion little glass pieces and was completely useless. Everyone looked at it and literally everyone was in tears.

Everyone knew that all JETLAX 4000 hopes and dreams were destroyed. Mike was dizzy. This was too much for him to take at once. This had to be an unforgettable day in a good way, not a bad way.
Months of day and night hard work all destroyed in a day. Only about 5 minutes later Mike realized something. All this devastation ultimately meant that LSRO would definitely be shut down. This meant that thousands of people would lose their jobs. Mike knew that he also would lose his job. There was literally no way that LSRO could recover from such a loss. This was worth 97 percent of the company's value.
This mission was going so well and everything was

destroyed.

Someone there had already called the cops because Mike heard some sirens and was sure that they were the cops. Everyone was aimlessly wandering around the headquarters. There were cops and news reporters all around. Mike was anchored next to the rocket that stood on the primary launchpad. He was looking at it for an hour and a half now.

He slowly walked close to it. He put a hand on it. If everything had gone according to plan, people would have been celebrating by now and most importantly his CEO would have been with him now. Mike started to tear up again. He knew that the huge mass that stood in front of him would soon be broken down.

Most people started leaving the headquarters. Mike figured that he would do the same. But he had a strange feeling that this was all preplanned. Although the cops took over the whole situation and Mike need not be involved, he had a strange feeling that all this that happened and the hole in his shoe might have some connection.

Mike eventually reached the parking lot where he found his car parked there. He somehow thought even the car felt disappointed for what just happened. Usually, whenever Mike would approach the car he would sense the car's big and bold stance. Now it somehow just looked quiet and subtle. He got into the car and left. He reached home and went in. He did not speak a single word to anybody after the incident. The last time he had spoken was to Katie in his office. He got in, threw his blazer on the couch and went on to take a shower.

He spent the rest of his day in a deep depression. He did not eat nor did he sleep. He just cried all day. Eventually, Sarah came home. She came home much earlier than usual. She had seen what happened on the news. She saw Mike lying on the couch. She went over to him. She knew he would not be in the mood to talk but he had too. He was already depressed and not talking will only make matters worse.

"Hey, I heard about what happened. I know you are devastated but you have to snap out of it", said Sarah.

"It is easier said than done", replied Mike.

Sarah could understand. This was no small incident. This was a massive accident. She left him alone after that. Days passed and so did weeks and eventually months. The police were still investigating who could have done this. Some experts said that it could have been one person but others say it had to be a group. The murder and the destruction of the HASRET had been planned so perfectly that there was literally no clue left behind. Mike thought of joining another space research organization and briefly also considered starting up his own but he did neither. He decided to stay at home and do some research, help out Sarah and have fun for the rest of his life. He had earned more than enough money to support him and his family for more than a lifetime.

He figured he would just take long vacations and road trips. He also decided to fulfill his dream of visiting every country in the world and staying in each country for at least two weeks. He had worked very hard for the first few years of his career and deserved a long break. He could always find a job later especially given his education, finding a job later should be a breeze.

He had totally forgotten about Brandon Lync and LSRO. He had also forgotten about the time when he wondered if there was any connection between the death of Brandon Lync and the hole in his shoe. Little did he know that he was what he had thought was true.

CHAPTER 4: THE SAFARI

Mike and Sarah were at terminal 4 of the airport. They were flying a far distance but it was all going to be worth it. Mike and Sarah were finally getting married.

Soon they boarded the flight. They flew for 5 hours straight and landed. It was 17th February and their wedding was to be held on the 22nd. A lot of guests had come over and finally, it was the wedding day. The wedding was grand, very grand. It was almost like a reality TV show.
Although there were a lot of people invited, the whole event itself ran smoothly. Mike and Sarah were finally married. They flew back and after a few months, things were back to as usual. Sarah's business was running very smoothly. Mike did not join any company yet but he was passionately traveling the world. He had visited 96 countries and was already planning on the 97th country.

A couple of years passed and it was 2022. Mike and Sarah had an 11 months old son named Grayson

Hensworth.

The investigation on Brandon Lync's case was briefly halted in 2021 but now was resumed in 2022. The only thing that the investigation team had discovered was that the entire murder was done by a single person only.

Mike had already visited most of the countries in the world. He had initially planned on staying in each county for at least two weeks but he soon figured it was way too much. He now stayed in each country for only about a day or two. A lot of times he would fly a long distance with a bunch of layovers in between.

Mike was sitting in the business class seat of the airbus a380 that was heading to Cairo. He had been longing to visit Cairo for more time than he can remember. This was actually a dream come true for Mike. It was a 7-hour flight. He had enjoyed the flight a lot. He always enjoyed flying. There was a cab waiting for him just outside the Cairo International Airport. The heat hit Mike as soon as he stepped out of the airport. This was by far the hottest place that Mike had ever traveled to. He found the driver of the car holding a board with his name written on it. Mike went over to him.

"Good afternoon sir, I believe you are Mike Hensworth", he said.

"Yes that is me", replied Mike. "Then follow me sir, and welcome to Cairo", said the driver.

Mike and the driver walked up to a black BMW 7-series parked in the parking lot. The driver went up the rear door and opened it. Mike did not see the driver unlock the car but he assumed that he would have unlocked it when Mike wouldn't have looked. As Mike entered the car he saw the hotel's name on the side of the car; INTERCRANE LUX.

The traffic was much worse than what Mike had anticipated. He knew there would be a lot of traffic but never thought it would take this long. A drive that should not have taken more than 15 minutes took more than three hours. Eventually, they reached the hotel. The hotel was pretty luxurious. It was late afternoon now and Mike decided to spend the rest of the day in the hotel itself and go into the desert the next day. He got to his room and went straight into the shower and spent about an hour and a half in there. He came out and took the time to look around. The room was very big. This was the top of the line room in INTERCRANE LUX. He had paid 8,768 Egyptian pounds for his room. But it was worth it. For starters the room was huge. It did not even look like a room. There was a massive living room equipped with a huge TV. There were five ultra-comfortable recliners in the living room. There were two different bedrooms. Both extremely furnished and well equipped with technology.

After the shower, Mike went to bed. He slept all the way to dinner time. Five minutes after he woke up, he got a call on the intercom. It was the receptionist.

"Good evening Mr. Mike, my name is Cane Blester, I hope you are having an amazing stay", she said. "Would you like to eat dinner now?" she asked.

"Yes sure", replied Mike.

"Would you like it served in your room or are you willing to come down?" she asked.

"I will come down", replied Mike and hung up. He sat there doing nothing for a minute. Then he picked up his phone. He went to the contacts and called Sarah. It was a video call. The phone rang a few times and got connected. The first thing Mike saw was Grayson smiling. That immediately put a smile on Mike's face. Then Sarah appeared. Mike spoke to Sarah for a while and then hung up. He quickly got changed and went down for dinner. The dinner area was really good. Next to the dining area, there was an enormous heated infinity pool where about 2 men and 1 family were hanging out. He went to the dining area. It was a buffet system. Mike had recently eaten a lots food in lots of different countries but he had never eaten food that tasted this good.

He ate almost everything but he especially liked the egg yolk ravioli and the deviled eggs with crab and caviar. After he finished eating, he sat by the pool for about half an hour and then got into it. The pool felt amazing to Mike. Especially considering how cold it gets at night in Cairo, the heated pool was a gift. He stayed in the pool for at least two hours before he got out. He was extremely tired. He went to his room and went straight to bed. The next morning the morning rays of the Cairo sun woke him up. He purposely left the curtains open the night before because he wanted to wake up this way.

He went into the bathroom, brushed his teeth, took a shower and got ready for the desert safari that he had planned and booked. He had been dreaming of this safari for years. He had always wanted to do this. His time had finally come. He was enjoying Cairo until now and he anticipated that this safari would also be a blast.

He was to go on this safari with Rahul Velan, a south Indian who he had met the day before. Mike had met Rahul the day before and invited him along the journey.

Mike got dressed and went down to the lobby. Rahul was waiting for him at the lobby. Both of them gave each other a casual hug and both of them walked out. There was a khaki colored jeep waiting in the parking lot. There was a driver inside and as soon as he saw them, he stepped out.

"Hello sir, my name is Rado and I will be your safari guide for today. Looks like you got a friend along with you", he said.

"Hello, yes I did!" replied Mike.

"Well hop on then, both of you have a long day ahead", he said in a cheerful voice as he got into the driver's seat.

Mike and Rahul got into the jeep. It was a bumpy, 2-hour long ride. They finally reached the beginning of the desert. Mike was fascinated. So was Rahul. Neither of them had seen such a wonder in their life.

The sand was a glowing gold colour and the very air felt sandy. All that could be seen was miles and miles of sand and sand dunes. The guide turned back.

"Ok listen up!" he snapped. He sounded very confident. "Just to recap, both of you will get off right over here head west for about seven and a half miles where I will be waiting for you. Both the backpacks that you guys have plenty of water, energy bars, two compasses, a knife, and the backpacks also have a GPS tracker with an inbuilt SOS button which you can press if you guys are in an extreme emergency situation and help will arrive in no more than two minutes. Also, your bags contain a couple of expandable walking sticks and finally a camera that you can use to take pictures. I will drive along the curvature of your path and meet you there. Be safe and have fun!" he said. As soon as he finished speaking he got into the jeep and drove off.

Mike and Rahul were left there alone with a slight breeze pushing their hair in all directions.

"Well I guess this is it", said Rahul. "Yeah I think so", replied Mike.

Mike reached for the compass in the bag. He took it out and opened it, and they started heading in the west direction.

Both of them were walking pretty fast. They enjoyed the walk. They were about 45 minutes in when they decided to take a break. They opened their bag and surprisingly wound a mat. Rahul took his mat out and laid it on the sand while Mike made a makeshift roof from the other mat to protect them from the heat. Although they were wearing hats, the makeshift roof made a big difference in controlling the heat. Rahul took out a water bottle and chugged it dry. Mike did the same but took the whole drinking process much slower. Both of them ate a couple of energy bars.

They were just sitting there when they strangely felt the wind grow stronger and stronger. At first, both of them thought that this was normal but the wind just kept getting stronger. And before they knew it they were stuck in a sandstorm. The wind was horrifying for both. Both of them stumbled to their feet and were grabbing their backpacks. But it was just too late. The wind pushed a bunch sand into their eyes. Rahul screamed as he was in agonizing pain. Both of them dropped their backpacks. Both of them were being pushed around like crazy by the wind. They lost track of everything. After about two minutes the harsh wind stopped. Both of them were stunned and speechless. This was totally out of the blue. They were covered in sand from head to toe.

"Mike, Mike he…he…help me please", said Rahul in a broken voice.

Mike turned to Rahul only to be shocked. One of the pocket knives was buried deep into Rahul's left chest. There was blood everywhere in his shirt.

Mike did not know what to do. He tried reaching for the SOS button but that was when he realized that the backpack was missing. Mike reached for the knife and tried to pull it out. No way, it would hurt way too much to bear. Mike literally could not think. He was in way too much pain himself. There was a bunch of sand in his eyes and he could barely see. He could not even wash his eyes as the bag got carried away by the wind. And the worst part of all this was they were lost in the middle of the desert without any help and no clue of the direction. As he was looking for some solution for this dreadful problem, he heard Rahul gasp. Mike turned around. Rahul called Mike towards him. Mike ran to Rahul. Rahul started speaking in a low, slow and painful voice. "Mike, please listen. There is absolutely no way you can save me after this. I am in agonizing pain right now. I know this is cruel but pull the knife out from my chest and cut my neck. This is the only way to end my suffering. Please." Mike could not believe what he just heard. "No way, get stupid thoughts out of your mind!"

Mike now suddenly sounded angry. "You are going to live. Do you understand? Just hang on, I will figure something out." Mike was shouting at the top of his voice at this point not only because the wind noises were pretty loud but also he did not want Rahul to drift off unconscious. Mike spent about a minute and then slowly started losing hope. Eventually, he lost all his hope. Then suddenly he turned to Rahul. Rahul knew that he was considering what he had said. Yes, Mike had to do it. Rahul was in too much pain and he really would not survive for more than five minutes.

The only sensible thing to do was put Rahul out of his misery. Mike started walking towards Rahul. Mike eventually reached Rahul. Mike was trembling. Rahul nodded his head ever so slightly giving him the final acknowledgment for his death.

Mike slowly reached for the knife in his chest. He was shivering more than ever. Mike's wrist was tightly wrapped around the knife. Then he finally did it. He closed his eyes pulled it as if he showed no mercy towards Rahul. Rahul shouted louder than ever. Now Mike was ready for the kill. He put the knife to Rahul's neck, ready for the kill. But he stopped. He started to think of things that were irrelevant. The image of his son just flashed before him. He thought of what this would make him as a person. Would this make him a killer? What would his wife think of him if she gets to know what he had done? He was in a big dilemma. His eyes settled on Rahul. Rahul looked like he already accepted his death. Mike finally gathered the courage to do it.

"Goodbye Mike, thank you for everything", said Rahul. Mike did not have the nerve to respond. And then he was ready for it. Mike closed his eyes and counted down from three in his mind. 3...2...1... then he did it. One single swipe and Rahul fell flat on the sand and stayed still.
Mike saw the blood seep into the sand, turning the sand deep red in color.

CHAPTER 5: NEW AND DANGEROUS

Mike was now stranded alone in a desert with literally no communication, water, shelter, and food. This was the worst thing that could ever happen. He briefly considered waiting where he was until Rado realizes that he was missing but Mike knew that he would be dead long before help arrives. The worst part was he did not know where to go. He looked at Rahul's body one last time and started walking aimlessly. He promised himself that if he got out of this alive he would come back and retrieve Rahul's body to at least give him a proper funeral so his soul may rest in peace.

Mike walked continuously for about half an hour and was in extreme need of water. He had a terrible headache due to dehydration and was on the verge of fainting. He tried his best to stay conscious because he knew that if he fainted that would be the end of him.

He kept walking and walking for about 2 hours and all of a sudden he stumbled on something.

He got up and checked what it was. It was a rock looking thing that was completely covered with sand. He put his hand on it and it sent a painful shock through his arm. He was thrown back but he got back to the rock. He looked around for something that he could pick it up with but all he could see was miles and miles of sand dunes.

And after about 20 seconds the idea struck. Mike immediately got to his feet. He removed his shoelace and then his shoe. He was wearing thick, rubbery hiking boots that were given to him by Rado. Then he put both his arms in the two shoes kind of using them as makeshift gloves. Then he picked it up. All the sand fell off it revealing a blue, shiny stone that was about the size of a human head. Mike was astonished. He had never seen anything like it although for a brief second it reminded him of the HASRET. He held it in his hands for a couple of seconds before he smelt something weird. The rock was emitting a citrusy smell that Mike could recognize as the smell of a lemon or an orange. The smell was kind of good. But then all of a sudden Mike felt something trickle down his nose. He dropped the rock and removed his right hand from the boot and touched his nose. Mike was shocked by what he saw. It was blood. Mike immediately knew that it was from the citrus smell emitted by the rock. He backed away. He thought for a minute and then he removed his jacket and threw it at the rock and covered it completely. Sure enough, the smell stopped. He immediately knew this was no ordinary rock. He put his hand back into the boot and picked it up without uncovering the jacket that was on the rock. He started walking with the rock in his hand. Eventually, the bleeding from his nose stopped but he was very much in need of water. Then, all of a sudden he made a 90 degree right turn and continued to walk. Then, to his surprise, after walking for about 25 minutes he saw Rado's jeep but it was still very, very far away. Mike shouted at the top of his voice but the effort went in vain. He continued moving towards the jeep. He got closer and shouted at the top of his voice. This time Rado heard him.

Rado was extremely shocked to see Mike. He immediately got into the jeep and drove straight to Mike. As soon as he reached Mike, he got off the jeep and helped Mike into the jeep. Mike picked up the closest water bottle he could find and literally finished the 2-liter bottle in a couple of gulps. Mike took a minute to gather all these thoughts and go through everything that happened in the past 2 hours. Then finally Rado spoke. "What happened, mate?" Mike explained everything. Although Rado saw the rock, he did not ask nor did Mike speak about it. Rado got into the jeep and started driving without speaking another word. Mike guided him on the way that he just came and they eventually found Rahul's body. It was covered in the sand completely. Mike went over to the body. He was already tearing up. Mike turned over the body. The face was horrible. All the blood had drained out and the face was horribly pale. Rado joined Mike at the scene. Rado did not show any expression. Both of them picked up the body and walked over to the jeep. They slowly placed the body on the rear seat. At this point, both Mike and Rado both were crying big time, Mike more than ever. Rado and Mike both sat at the front of the jeep and started to drive away. They went to the hotel, collected all his information and called his family. In a couple of days, the funeral was over, just as Mike had promised. Mike never mentioned the rock to anyone. Mike took the rock back home in a private jet that he hired as this would be impossible to hide through security if he were to travel in a commercial airplane.

Mike was back at home. He had hidden the rock in his basement in a place that literally no one would ever think of looking. There was a false tile at the end of the basement that Mike had made himself when the house was built. Mike knew the rock was dangerous. He wanted to do some research about it before he even opened the tile.

It was about 5 days since he returned from Cairo and forgot about it for a couple of days. The first thing that Mike did was to check the periodic table. He checked each and every element in the periodic table and the characteristics of each element. He spent days and nights checking each and every element. Once he was done, he was shocked. Not even one

element showed any resemblance to the one he had found. Mike was totally confused. That was when Mike heard the knock on the door.
Mike immediately put away his research papers and pulled out the novel that he was pretending to read. Mike did not want Sarah to know about this.

"Come in", said Mike. The door opened and Sarah appeared. "Hey, what are you doing?" she asked. "Nothing, just reading this novel", said Mike.

"Great, I got you your coffee and remember, Grayson is asleep so if you have any plans of booming out Michael Jackson music in the living room Mr. Mike, just forget it", said Sarah. She sounded funny and she smiled at Mike. Mike smiled back. Sarah walked to the table, placed the coffee down on the table and left. Mike sighed. He felt like he should tell Sarah about this but he knew that he would unnecessarily drag Sarah into this. Mike Was now confused. He was actually pretty confident that this would be some element in the periodic table but now he feared the worst. He felt that he had just discovered a new element. It also made some sense to Mike as he knew that the desert in which he went for the safari wasn't explored entirely and more than 60 percent of the desert was unexplored. And Mike thought that when he got lost he
would have gotten into some of the unexplored areas of the desert. Mike knew this was big. This rock was extremely dangerous. Mike wanted

to tell someone about this. And then it sparked in his mind. He knew the exact man who was trustworthy enough. Jake Camber was the man.
Mike pulled out his phone. Mike's hands were shaking. He called Jake.

"Hey Jake, Jake, Jake listen please, please listen", Mike was panicking. "Hey what happened?" Jake sounded sleepy. Mike checked the time; it was 1:30 am. Mike was disappointed with himself. He had been worrying for so long that he was now losing his sleep. And worst of all he was now dragging someone else into the mess he was in.

"Jake, listen up. I want to meet you first thing in the morning. What time should I come to your house?" Mike asked.

"Umm, maybe at 8 in the morning", replied Jake. He sounded more awake now. "Ok I will be there by 8", said Mike and hung up.
Only after hanging up Mike realized how sleepy he was. Mike went to sleep on the bed next to the study table. Mike passed out like a baby.

The next morning Mike woke up pretty early at 6:30 am. Mike got up and went to his bathroom and showered really quickly. He had newer showered this fast before. Mike went up from the basement to the living room. Mike saw Sarah sitting on the couch sipping on her morning coffee. "Whoa, you are up early today", said Sarah. "Yeah, I got somewhere to be", said Mike. Mike was still very tired and Sarah could make it out of the way he spoke. "You sound tired", she said. "Yeah…..I did not exactly sleep properly last night; the novel was too interesting to stop. Okay, anyway, I got to go", said Mike as he was heading to the main door. "Bye Bye", said Sarah and Mike left.

It was a 45-minute drive to Jake's house. Thankfully there was no traffic on the road. Jake was on his front porch waiting for Mike. Then came Mike. Jake was happy to see Mike. They hadn't seen each other for a while. Mike arrived in his Chiron. Mike got down and ran to Jake. He did not utter a word nor did he allow Jake too. Mike pulled him by his jacket and threw him in the passenger seat of this car. Mike got into the driver's seat and drove off. Mike then started to speak. Mike told him everything that happened from safari to the funeral. Jake was speechless. This was too much for Jake to digest. Jake was speechless. Jake responded with "Ok, what now?" They were still traveling but they were just a couple of minutes away from the house.

"I do not know", said Mike. Then both of them were silent until they reached the basement of Mike's house. Mike walked to the false tile and opened it. Jake saw a ball-shaped thing covered with a thick blanket.
Jake was tempted to take the blanket off but he knew that would instantly get both of them killed. "This is it", said Mike. "Yeah……." said Jake as he was

staring at it.

"I don't know about this Mike, this is too hard to believe. We lost our jobs from LSRO, got our boss killed, and now this!" said Jake. "How about we put this back where you found it and forget all this even happened." "Are you kidding me Jake!?" said Mike. "Do you have any idea about how dangerous this is? This literally gave me a shock and made my damn nose bleed!" Mike boomed. Jake knew that what Mike said was correct. This was pretty dangerous. Just as both of them were thinking about what they were going to do, Jake got a call. It was an unknown number. Jake answered the call. The person speaking on the other end was very serious. He had an African accent.

"Am I speaking to Mr. Jake Camber?" the voice said. "Yes, this is Jake Camber," said Jake. "I am the head of the investigation team working on Brandon Lync's murder case. We think we know who the murderer is", said the voice.

"What? Who is it?" asked Jake. "I'm sorry sir but this is highly confidential and cannot be discussed over the phone. I would suggest you come to the investigation center right now", said the voice. "I'm on my way", Jake said and hung up.

Jake told Mike what he heard and Mike was speechless. Without uttering another word, both of them ran to the garage. They got into the Chiron and Mike drove crazy fast. Mike almost hit 3 cars on the way but he did not care. He wanted to know who was responsible. Soon, they reached the investigation center. Mike and Jake went in and introduced themselves. The head of the investigation introduced himself as Arron Atzen.

"We gathered up all the clues and we finally, for sure, know who the murderer is. It is Clanton Ruder", said Arron.
"What? Why would he do it?" asked Mike. "Who's Clanton?" asked Jake. "Clanton Ruder is the CEO and founder of SpaceRun, another private space research organization just like LSRO. Both of them were founded at the same time but SpaceRun did not do too well in this field. You might have not even heard SpaceRun as it really did not do too well in the space research field", said Mike. Jake was taking all of this in.
The entire place was silent for about a minute. Then Arron spoke, "We know for a fact that it was Clanton Ruder who murdered him. But we just could not get hold of him and I am afraid that we never will."

"But why?" asked Jake.

"He left the country and we have no clue where he is", answered Arron.

Mike swore. He really wanted to have Clanton dead. Mike was raging with anger. Mike then said goodbye to Arron and left. Mike went home and went straight into the shower. He went to bed but could fall asleep easily. After about just lying on the bed for about 3 hours, Mike finally managed to fall asleep.

He went on with his life as nothing happened on the outside. But on the inside, he was permanently shattered.

PART: 2

THE PRESENT...

YEAR: 2080

CHAPTER 1: THE BEST AGENT

The man in the black jacket was the head of the group. The car chase was massive. Around 20 police cars were on the chase behind a stolen BMW prototype 17 that was speeding on the freeway. The man in the BMW prototype 17 was one of the most wanted men alive. But the man in the black coat was calm, cool and collected.

"Alpha team 204 go to your left and cover-up", said the man on the radio. The man was in the passenger front seat of the first police car in the chase. He turned to the driver and told him to turn right."

"But sir, the target is going through the left road", said the driver. "Just go!" replied the man. The driver said as he was told. The driver was an intelligent man too. Nobody was selected into the crime hunt team unless they were the absolute best. But in this case, the driver knew the man sitting next to him was in charge and he knew what he was doing.

The man in charge was called Matten

Hensworth, the son of Grayson Hensworth.

The Alpha team 204 went to the left road and blocked the target while Matten Hensworth was speeding to the right. The driver was still confused but he did not question Matten because the driver knew that whatever he did was for a reason.

The Alpha team had managed to block the target and just as Matten had anticipated. Then again just as Matten had anticipated, the target turned right and the target was now on the bridge. Then the driver understood the plan and without even receiving instructions from Matten, he turned left and now he was on the other end of the bridge. Now the target was trapped with police cars on either side of the bridge. That was when Matten's car came to a skidding halt and Matten jumped out of the car with a single semi-automatic pistol in his hand. He took about 4 seconds to aim and took 1 shot at the car speeding towards him. Even before the bullet went through the windshield, he knew he got the perfect shot. The bullet hit the target in the middle of the forehead and he was dead spot on. Matten had the shooting order and used it without any hesitation.

The BMW flew off the side of the bridge at hit the water flat. The retrieving team was already on their way. Matten walked back to the car. The driver was astonished but said nothing. 15 minutes later the team was back at the base. As usual, Matten had done it. Matten was the best agent that ACH, Alpha

Crime Hunt had ever recruited. The only thing that made Matten different from others was the fact that he wasn't scared at all. Nothing in this world could scare him. He had no family whatsoever. He wasn't married and his parents had died in a car accident.

Alpha had provided him with an exclusive Audi prototype made specifically for him which he could drive manually also along with auto- drive. Only the Alpha agents could have cars with the self drive. All other cars were completely automated.

He was congratulated at the Alpha base as usual. He was hands down the best head and the crime operator was the closest person he knew at the base. The Alpha base was huge. The base was 98 percent automated. There were robots everywhere and very few people to be seen. This was a new era. Most of the complicated jobs had been replaced by robots. Cars like Rolls-Royce Phantom had now become vintage cars.

Matten was a master of intelligence. Like his grandfather Mike Hensworth, he was also known for thinking like no one else.

Matten's work for the day was over. He stepped on his hoverboard. Unlike hoverboards in the past, hoverboards in 2080 were completely in the air. He selected the destination on the hoverboard as 'parking lot'.

The hoverboard carried him to the parking lot where his car was parked. He got off the hoverboard and went over to the car. The car sensed Matten through a number of ways and unlocked even before he reached the car. Matten got in and sat on the inbuilt couch in the car. The car was sized like a large 4 seater and had a couch in the rear of the car just like any other car but he also had another captain's chair on which he can sit and drive manually. But this time Matten did not drive. He got in and said the one word 'home' and car drove away. The ETA said that he would reach home in 14 minutes 34 seconds and he reached in exactly that time. The technology was precise to the second.

While almost everyone in the world had moved to automated houses, Matten still lived in his grandfather's house. Matten wasn't really a big fan of all this automation. Although he was born in an era in which technology ruled, he secretly wished that he had been born in his grandfather's era.

Matten lived alone and really liked his house. Matten was not a very emotional person but he had been extremely curious about what was inside the basement of his house. Matten's parents had told him that the basement had been locked since his grandfather's time and no one had opened it before as it was his grandfather's room and everyone decided it will stay that way. Mike had never met his grandfather but he had heard a lot of stories about him and he really loved his grandfather although he had never met him before.

Matten took a quick shower after he got home.

Matten was 25 years old and extremely fit. He was arguably the fittest person in the Alpha team. Matten lived in an era where people were just not fit. Every house had a robot that did essential chores around the house and people got lazier and lazier over the past 2 decades.

Matten came out of the shower and got dressed in comfy nightclothes. When he was about to get to the bed to watch some TV, he got a call. It was the crime operator from the Alpha base. Matten answered the call in just a couple of rings. Then a hologram came on. Now the operator was facing Matten in a life-size form and he looked pretty serious. He hologram was wearing a black suit and a golden tie with shades on.
Then he removed the shades.

"Hello Matten, where are you right now?" asked the crime operator. His name was Barry Bells.

"Hey Barry, I'm at home. How else do you think I'll be talking to you? Why what's up?" asked Matten.

"The person you killed today was the leader of a criminal organization called FORECLAW. They are a multinational criminal organization and are very angry with you. You can expect anything bad coming up." said Barry.

"Come on Barry, you think I give a damn about it. Let them come, I'll try and shoot them down if I can't then that will be time to say goodbye. I honestly do not care", said Matten.

"Honestly Matten, I think you should care about your life a tad bit more", requested Barry.

"Chill bro, I'm fine", said Matten.

"Ok then, take care and goodbye", said Barry and hung up.
Mike was then about to go to bed when he felt like he wanted to watch some TV and slept on the couch.

The next morning Matten woke up at 6 am and went jogging for about an hour. Then he ordered a double beef deck burger from a local burger shop. In about 7 minutes, the burger arrived. There were a notification and Matten went to the door. There was a robot to deliver the burger and he snatched it from the robot. He did not like robots much. He ate the burger quickly and left to work. He went over the pending cases for the whole day and before he knew it, the time was over 11 pm. That was when he left to go home. Matten drove manually because the road was empty and he could drive really fast. He reached home in a couple of minutes. His car was capable of hitting speeds of up to 335 miles per hour. He was at the door, scanning his palm when he heard it. He heard a huge bang. He looked up and saw that about 4 missiles were heading to his house. One had already hit the roof and his roof was on fire.
Even worse he realized only a second later. One of the missiles was heading straight to Matten. Matten immediately got off to a run. He was

extremely fit and could run very fast but this time he just could not run fast enough. The missile hit the ground about 20 meters away from Matten and the shockwave sent Matten flying into the river 10 meters away. Matten already knew this was all from FORECLAW. There were more missiles from some jetpack robots circling around his house in the sky. They were sending missiles after missiles and his house was getting bombarded. The house was a very strong house but there was no way it could withstand such missiles. For the first time in many years, Matten started to tear up. This was his grandfather's house. And now it was all gone in an instant. Matten was angry up to a point where he was shaking. He wanted to punch the man responsible for death. Matten knew he had to calm down. Matten looked for his HC (Hologram Communicator) in his pocket. Matten looked for it in his front jeans pocket but it wasn't there. Matten thought that he had lost it in the blast but then he remembered that he had put it in his back pocket when he was back at work. He reached for it in his back pocket and sure enough it was there. He swam to the shore of the river. He called Barry immediately. As the phone was ringing, Matten heard the cops roll into the blast scene. Then the call connected. A small holographic image of Barry lifted off the screen.

"Matten, I just heard about what happened. Gosh, are you alright?" asked Barry.

"Yes, I'm fine. I want to burn the hell out of FORECLAW", Matten was furious. More than anything it was the sight of his grandfather's house burn down that hurt him the most.

"Matten just calms down, you focus on getting to a safe place. I'll be there in an hour", said Barry. Then he hung up.

Matten looked up and he saw that the jetpack robots had disappeared. The damage had been done. Matten was confident that the new head of FORECLAW thought that he was dead.

Matten looked front again and gasped. It was one of the humanoid robots from the fire and rescue team and the robot was lending him a hand. Matten drew a deep breath and reached out of the robot's hand. The robot pulled him out and ran to the ambulance.

Matten was given some first aid and then he was left alone. He walked up to a nearby bench and went over what had just happened. It all happened too quickly to believe. But he knew it was true. There was a part of him that wished all this was just a bad dream.

Matten looked around and took in everything that was happening around him.
He saw multiple people running in all directions. A huge number of robots were fighting to put off the fire. There were a few aerial flying machines

that were spraying water and powdered dry ice on the house. There were multiple police cars already present there and many more were rolling into the scene. Matten saw the whole scene go black for a second and before he knew it, he was asleep.

CHAPTER 2: THE RE-DISCOVERY

Matten woke up on a stretcher near his burnt down house. Most of the people had gone and there were a few fire-robots running around.
Matten turned and saw Barry sitting next to him. Barry noticed that he was awake and offered him some water. Matten finished the whole bottle.

"Well….now I'm officially homeless", said

Matten jokingly. "Don't worry. Our team is

already on the hunt for the new

FORECLAW head. They will find him sooner or later. Now go inside and see if any of your valuables survived. Get them and let's get to my house. You can stay there for a while until you get the interiors done in your new house. The work is already underway. Your new house is a couple of blocks away from here. I've already sent you the interior design on your hologram. If you want any design changes, you can directly contact the interior designer. I must add your new house is going to be 90 percent automated", said Barry.

"Oh no…" said Matten.

"I tried my best but that was the least amount of automation they could include in the house. Including more and more automation just makes their construction easier", replied Barry.

"It's OK, chill. I got to be grateful for you for making all this effort for me. Thanks a lot", said Matten.

Then both of them were silent for about 2 minutes. Then Matten got up and walked to the remains of his house. Matten was inevitably tearing up. He went through the remains of the door. He wiped his tears and went into the house. He looked around. He could make out the hallway and other ways but nothing looked like it looked before. Everything was black with soot and everything was burnt. Matten could not recollect anything that would be important. He thought of some important Alpha plans and charts but he knew all that would have been burnt to ashes.

He sighed and turned to leave when he heard the creaky noise of a door slowly open. That was when it struck Matten. It was the basement door. It was finally open. He ran down the stairs and saw that the basement door was half-open. He ran in at that very instant. He was extremely shocked to see that nothing in the room was burnt or damaged because the room held up pretty well and the only thing that broke was the door lock. Matten saw that the basement was huge. It was extremely dusty though. Matten saw multiple papers that looked like some sort of research paper. He picked it up and saw a word written in large and bold handwriting – CLANTONIUM. He read everything that was written on the sheets of paper. Although they were old and yellow, the letters were still very legible. Matten started reading the papers. Matten read it for two minutes and that was when he read something that shocked him. He went completely speechless. He looked like he just saw something haunted. Matten was completely speechless when he heard Barry call out his name. Matten immediately placed the papers on the table and started to behave as if nothing had happened.

"Matten…..Matten where are …. Whoa what is this place", said Barry as he walked into the basement.

"I know right. This place is so cool. This was my grandfather's study supposedly", said Matten.

Matten thought of hiding the paper that he found but he thought it would be right if he told Barry about it.

"Barry, look what I found", said Matten as he picked up the papers that he placed on the table and handed it to Barry.

But as he started reading the papers, Matten

picked out the paper that shocked him the most. Barry started reading it.

'It's extremely dangerous...........Nose bleeds.........shock through my hand..........false tile...Clanton Ruder...The HASRET Brandon Lync was killed for entry of the vault...But, Ruder is still out there and depending on the time you find this, maybe even his grandson.'

Barry was speechless. Matten was staring at Barry.

"And the worst part is...The so-called newly discovered element Clantonium, is in this room", said Matten. Both Matten and Barry turned to the false tile as mentioned in the paper. Barry walked up to it. Barry pressed the tile and it popped up. Barry looked at Matten and Matten nodded his head for acknowledgment. Barry was about to lift it up when he saw a few breathing masks placed next to the false tile.

Barry picked up a couple and tossed one to Matten and he wore one himself. Matten understood what that was for and wore it immediately. If not he would probably bleed to death. Then Barry lifted the tile and there it was. The element was covered with a thick blanket which surprisingly was pretty dust free. Matten guessed that the tile was really good at protecting what lay inside. Barry uncovered the blanket and there it was. The blue and shiny element that Matten's grandfather had named CLANTONIUM. Barry was tempted to pick it up but he knew that such an action might result in death.

"Well, this is it", said Barry. "Yes, but it is just a beginning of something big", said Matten is a very serious and deep voice. Both Matten and Barry walked out and were going over what they had just witnessed. Barry pulled out a cigar and started to smoke on it. That was, in fact, the only minus point of Barry. But now his addiction was much lesser than a few years ago. He used to smoke at least 5 times a day but now he had gotten it down to just about one or two per week.

Matten pulled out his hologram and tuned on the news. He really liked to watch the news. He would have preferred physical newspapers but now they were a thing of the past. He slightly chuckled hopelessly when he saw the replay of yesterday's news of his house burning down. He was watching the news for about 10 minutes when he changed the channel to NASA. This was his favorite channel. According to Matten, NASA was the only thing existent on his hologram that gave him information that was actually useful to him. Matten saw that there was something that NASA was introducing something called the ELEMEASURE. They claimed that the newly invented device called ELEMEASURE measures the danger levels associated with all the elements. One of the world's most dangerous elements, Plutonium which is unimaginably dangerous and radioactive was measured 7.68 on the scale. Matten nudged Barry to grab attention.

He wanted Barry to see what he was watching and Barry did just that.

Barry was surprised by the coincidence. They had just supposedly discovered a new element and they found their way to proceed with their discovery. Both Matten and Barry looked at each other and they knew that they were thinking the same thing. Matten remembered the place written on the letter where his grandfather had written where he had found the piece of Clantonium. Both of them nodded at each other and they ran to Barry's car. They sat inside and Barry was driving to the airport while Matten searched his hologram for some last-minute flight tickets to Cairo. Matten was inevitably tearing up again he had remembered his car which he loved. But now it was no more after the missile attack. Matten had forgotten about the attack completely. All he
was thinking of now was the 'so-called Clantonium'. Luckily Matten found a flight in a couple of hours leaving for Cairo. There were three seats free and Matten booked all three. The hoped that an entire row would be allotted to Matten and Barry so they would be able to talk about this during the flight a little more openly. The tickets cost much more than if they were booked sometime before but Matten did not care.

It was an E-ticket. The ticket was sent to Matten's hologram. They reached the airport in less than 15 minutes. Most people of the Alpha team were provided with manual-drive cars. Barry was a very good driver and at the same time was very precise in his driving. He wasn't always like this. Driving skill was one of the training categories in the Alpha training. In a world where most people did not know how to drive, this training for driving was crucial. End even more important when you are going to be a part of the Earth's most secretive and efficient crime hunt group. They got into the terminal without any security checks because they showed their identity cards stored in their hologram.

The flight was very crowded. As they had wished they got an entire row to themselves. The flight felt short to both of them and they did not talk about this during the flight much. They landed in Cairo and it was unbelievably hot. The heat hit them as soon as they stepped out of the plane. They were almost running into the airport. They were relieved when they got to the airport. The finished all the immigration and now they had to step out of the airport. The heat hit them immediately but this time they were ready for it so it wasn't that bad of a surprise. Their cab was waiting for them, automated of course. They got into the car and the car started driving away. The destination was already set; Fairmont Nile City. Matten had booked the hotel in the flight for a little more usual but he did not mind at all. Clantonium was the only think on his mind. They reached the hotel in about 12 minutes as there was no traffic. Traffic was now a thing of the past. All cars moved in a systematic way as it was all autonomous. The distance was about 13.5 miles. They had booked one double top of the line room for them to stay. It would have taken about 12 hours 60 years ago to travel to Cairo but in this era, it took them just 3 hours for them to travel. Both of them were given a microchip at the reception by the receptionoid (humanoid robot as receptionist) which they injected into their palm and once they approach the door, it would unlock the door. There was also a face unlock feature at the door for people who did not want to inject the chip into their bodies. The chip was completely safe though. It would dissolve into the blood and the kidney would discard it through urine. It would not affect the body in any way whatsoever. Matten and Barry got to their room. Matten took a quick shower and Barry scrolled through some news in his hologram. They had booked the safari too. Matten had read the letter written by his grandfather clearly. Mike had written everything that happened and Matten smartly booked the most similar kind of safari in the same desert area. Both Matten and Barry knew that it wouldn't be easy to find the same place where Mike had found all this. They weren't even sure if it would be of any use of going there. The only reason they had come to Cairo was hoping they would find more pieces Clantonium. They planned to go the next day morning. Both Matten and Barry slept pretty early. They were extremely tired and they had to wake up early the next morning. They woke up early and got ready. They went down and saw a red-colored autonomous car waiting. They approached the car and the door opened automatically. They saw a huge screen in the car and as soon as they got in. There was a man wearing a white blazer on the screen. Somehow the dress he was wearing did not suit him. The man on the screen started speaking out and told them the guidelines on their trip. Matten guessed that it was all going to be the same as his grandfather's trip as all the guidelines were pretty much the same as what his grandfather had written in the letter. There was a little button next to the screen and Matten pressed that and the whole screen changed to a green color with the word start written on it. Matten anticipated that he had just skipped the introduction and he pressed start. The vehicle started moving and they were on their way to the moment of truth. Will they be able to find out whether there was more of Clantonium out there or that was the only piece? Barry knew that was a very low probability. There was no way an element would exist in just one small piece. They reached the safari spot. Matten was surprised to see that this place was actually not modernized. The desert looked the same as pictures from 60 years ago. Then they were off.

They walked and kept walking. They did not know where to go or where to search. The time was running out. The rescuebots will be on their way soon searching for these two. They had already been out here for a couple of hours. They knew what they were doing would not help at all. That was when they decided to split up. They had no way to get lost because they had their hologram with them. They had searched for a couple of hours but found no clue on Clantonium.

Matten was much more desperate than Barry. But soon Matten's hopes faded. Matten was about to call Barry when he suddenly stopped.
Something had caught his eye. He turned to this left and saw something shining under a thin layer of sand. He ran towards it as fast as he could. He thought he was just hallucinating but as he got closer and closer he saw that the shine grew a little brighter and brighter. Matten eventually got there. He brushed away sand and was taken aback. He was that what he found looked exactly like Clantonium. Even worse he thought that could be Clantonium itself. He moved a few steps back. He had clearly read what it can do to a human body. He pulled out his hologram and called Barry. Barry picked up and a 3D hologram of Barry popped up on Matten's hologram.

"Barry, come to me immediately", screamed Matten. "Ok sure", said Barry and hung up.

Barry looked for Matten's location on the hologram and ran there. Barry ran pretty fast and reached Matten in no time. Barry saw that Matten was crouching next to something that appeared to shine. Barry knew what it was. It had to be Clantonium. Barry joined Matten. Matten looked very serious.

"Whoa what the hell", said Barry. "Yeah I know right", said Matten. "Should we dig up more?" asked Barry.

"No", replied Matten. He thought for a minute and turned to Barry. "We'll get back to the hotel and pack our bags. We're leaving for Washington first thing tomorrow morning", said Matten.

CHAPTER 3: ELEMEASURE

They were back in the hotel room. They had called for the emergency rescue and they were lead back to their hotel room in the same car that they had come in. That night Matten had explained everything to Barry.

"Do you remember the thing that NASA was announcing the day we came?" asked Matten. "Yeah the measurement thing right?" replied Barry.

"Yeah the Elemeasure", said Matten. "You know what that machine is capable of right? It can measure the 'danger' involved in any element. I say we can just take Clantonium to them and we could learn a little more about Clantonium."

"Yeah, I think that is a good idea. I think that the information that NASA can provide us with will be extremely crucial for our understanding of Clantonium. But there is a problem. Do you think they will just let us go meet the head and tell them about Clantonium? Because what we say will just sound like it was out of a science fiction movie.

We won't even get past the front gate security if we try telling them this."

"Chill, we are the members of Alpha Crime Hunt. I'm confident that they will take this matter seriously."

And then they eventually went to bed. Matten had already booked the flight tickets for the next morning. The earliest flight he could find was at 11 am. Matten figured he would wake up pretty early and go for a jog before the hot and bright Cairo sun comes out. He knew that the air would not be the freshest in the world but he knew the pollution would be significantly lower in the early hours of the morning.

The next morning Matten woke up at 5 and went into the bathroom. He brushed and had a shower and he came out. Barry was awake when Matten came out of the bathroom. Barry was watching some 3D news on his hologram. He saw Matten come out of the bathroom.

"Good morning Matten", said Barry. "Good morning Barry. You are up early, what's the matter? Asked Matten. "I just got a call from Alpha. It looks like there is a glitch in the Crimetrac software. They wanted you to fix it. Looks like the robots are not helping in this matter", said Barry. "I knew those darn things were up to no good", said Matten. As soon as he finished saying that he heard a robotic voice in his room saying 'Delivery for Mr. Matten'. Matten turned to the screen next to the door that allowed him to see who was outside. It was one of those humanoid robots with something in its hand. "And here's another one of those darn things….." said Matten as he leaned to the bedside table and pushed a button. As soon as he pushed the button marked 'Main Door', the main door opened allowing the robot to walk in. It was carrying two cups of cappuccino. It walked all the way over to the dining table and placed the tray on the table. Matten than spoke to the robot.

"How did you know we were awake? Asked Matten.

"There is a weight sensor on your bed sir and I am connected to all the sensors in your room. Once I got notified that the weight on your bed reduced, I and programmed to get you the coffee", said the robot.

"What do you mean all the sensors? How many sensors are there?" asked Matten.

"There are a lot of sensors. Do you want me to name all of them?" the robot asked.
"No, it's fine. Just leave", commanded Matten.

"Thank you, sir, have a nice stay", said the robot and left the room. The main door automatically closed behind it.

"Gosh these creepy little things!" said Matten. "Anyway, I'm going for a run. Do you want to join me?"

"Yeah sure, I'll just go fresh up", said Barry and went

into the bathroom.

Matten went over to the dining table. He picked up a cup and started sipping on the coffee. He slowly walked back to the bed and sat on it. He pressed another button on the side table and the curtains opened.

The sun was not out yet and it was still dark. Matten just took the last sip of his coffee when Barry came out of the bathroom. Barry was already dressed in the sportswear that the hotel had provided for him. Barry went over to the dining table and almost chugged the coffee cup dry. The coffee stayed at the same temperature as when it was delivered as the coffee cup had an inbuilt heater that could keep the temperature constant even for days. Then both of them were ready to head out the door.

The hotel itself had a place to walk and jog but both Matten and Barry wanted to look around Cairo a little more. A couple of days ago even the thought of going for a jog in Cairo would have been irrelevant but now it was the reality. One advantage of being in the Alpha team was that you could fly to any part of the world, any time because visas and passports would already be taken care of as soon as you decide to fly somewhere. Coming to Cairo was no exception. The jogged close to the hotel itself. They had no worries about missing the flight because the hotel they were staying in provided an autonomous helicopter to take them to the airport. The jogged for about 2 hours and got back to the hotel. They took a quick shower and got ready for their flight. Matten had already paid for the hotel room so he directly went to the breakfast buffet. Both Matten and Barry ate some peanut butter and jelly sandwich. They also had some prickly pear juice to go along with the bread. Prickly pear was something that was available very easily in Cairo. Then they went up to the roof of the building. The helicopter was already waiting for them. There was not only one but there were 4 helicopters ready to take any passenger, anywhere, anytime. Matten and Barry got into the closest one. There was one curved sofa along with the rear cabin of the helicopter and nothing else except a large screen to the front of the cabin.

The helicopter took them to the airport in just a couple of minutes. Their visas and Passports were already ready. They got into the airports and as usual, were not bothered by security.

At exactly 11:05 am, they were on the flight to Washington. The plan was that Barry would go and book a good hotel to stay while Matten would go to his old house and bring Clantonium to Washington to show NASA.

Matten's grandfather's house was in New York. By an automated car, it would take about 3 hours to go from Washington to New York but Matten had already asked for a self-drive car from the Alpha group and they said that his new car

would be waiting for him at Washington Dulles International Airport for him. With a self-drive car, Matten could drive from Washington to New York in just 1hour and 35 minutes.
Also, he had no worries about anyone spotting Clantonium and raising questions about it.

The flight was pretty short and not very crowded. It took them about 3 hours to reach Washington. As promised, there was a self-drive BMW waiting for Matten and Barry in the Airport's parking lot. They walked up to the car and it unlocked automatically. Matten guessed that it would have been connected to his hologram. As they were getting into the car, Barry finally found a luxury hotel with rooms with the suites available. Barry booked a suite for two people immediately. Barry booked the suite at Trump International Hotel and Matten was now driving there. Matten dropped Barry off at the hotel and drove off to New York.

Barry watched Matten drive off super fast. It was only a few seconds before Matten's car disappeared out of sight.

"That's one fast dude", said Barry to himself as he walked into the hotel. The hotel looked strangely similar to their last one. Barry figured that even though the location was different, the technology was the same.
This hotel also had a similar approach to entry

and of the room. This hotel also provided a chip that people can inject into their bodies. Just like the previous one, this one was also completely harmless.

Barry noticed the first real difference when he stepped into his hotel room. This room was way more luxurious than the other one. It was more of a luxury apartment than a room. Barry did not have anything to do until the next day so he decided to take a long shower and sleep for a while. Barry was sleeping when his hologram buzzed. He woke up and gestured at the hologram and the 3D call was connected. It was Matten.

"Hey where are you?" asked Matten.

"Hey, I'm in the hotel room. Where are you?" asked Barry.

"I'm at the hotel and I wanted to know which room you are in. I figured I would ask you rather than those stupid robots", said Matten.

"Room number 106, the seventh floor", replied Barry.

"Ok thanks, I'll come up in

sec." "Sure, take your time."

Barry heard Matten walk up to the door and he opened it even before he could call him. Matten was wearing a black suit and weirdly he was wearing a backpack. Barry immediately knew what it was. It had to be the piece of Clantonium.

"Thanks for getting the door', said Matten.

"You bet", replied Barry. "What's that in your hand? Is that what I think it is?"

"As a matter of fact, it is. But there is no need to worry, it's protected very well", said Matten when he saw Barry slightly start to panic.

Matten looked around the room. He nodded his head for acknowledgment. "This is a pretty fancy room", he said.

Then he walked over to the dressing room and tucked away from the bag in a far corner. Barry looked at the time.

"It's an 8:30. Do you want to go down for dinner or should we get a robot to serve it here?" asked Barry.

"We'll go down. I heard this hotel has a good dining area. We could kill some time there and come back and go straight to bed." Replied Matten.

The Dining area was massive. The dining area was right next to the infinity pool. There were a good number of people but in no means was it crowded. There were absolutely no staff members at all. It was all handled by humanoid robots. Everything from serving the food all the way to maintenance was all taken care of by these robots. But the food was always cooked by a human chef. That was the food that was always a little customized to meet the preferences of the people eating the food.

Both Matten and Barry were both pretty hungry. They wanted to eat some barbequed meat for starters but they went out of control and filled themselves up with the starters itself. Both of them were too full for the main course so they decided to skip it and went directly to dessert.

Matten had a chocolate sundae and some chocolate truffles whereas Barry just had some vanilla bean ice cream.

Then they decide to go swimming. The pool was heated and it felt good. They spent a good amount of their time in the pool. They were very tired at the end of the swim. As planned, they took a shower when they got back and went straight to bed.

They woke up pretty early the next morning. Matten was the first to wake up. He woke up at around 5:30 am. Barry woke up soon after that at 6 am. Both of them showered and got ready. They had breakfast and were now ready for checkout. Barry was checking the room for anything that they might have left behind while Matten went to grab the bag that had Clantonium in it. He held the bag in his hand for a minute and went into some sort of deep thought. Barry noticed that.

"Matten", said Barry but there was no response. "Matten!" this time he said it much louder. Matten was confused for a second and then looked at Barry. "Yeah?" he said.

"Shall we leave?" asked Barry. He knew that Matten was thinking about his old house. He knew how much that house meant to him. That was his grandfather's residence. It was really near and dear to Matten's heart.
They then left the room. Barry had already paid for the room. Their car was in the parking lot. But this time neither of them drove. They got into the car and Barry spoke to the inbuilt assistant.

"Nester, navigate and drive to NASA headquarters", he said. "Sure, navigating and driving to NASA headquarters, Washington DC, Washington", replied Nester. Nester was the name of the voice assistant inbuilt into the car. The ETA was 4minutes 17seconds and they reached in exactly the given time.

The NASA headquarters was massive. The gate itself was pretty intimidating. The car automatically pulled over next to the gate. Both Matten and Barry got down. Matten had the backpack with him. They walked up to the gate. There were three robots at the gate; two at each side of the gate and one in a cubicle.

Barry spoke to the robot on the left side of the gate.

"Can I talk to a human?" asked Barry. "This is something very important."

"Sure sir, may I know the purpose of the visit?" asked the robot. The robot had an unusually robotic voice. The robot sounded like it was made in 2070.

"It's complicated! A metalhead like you won't understand", Matten interrupted. He sounded extremely angry. Barry turned to Matten. "Hey, calm down", Barry said. Matten did not respond. Matten tuned to the robot. "Just call an official", he said. "Contacting Miss Grena", said the robot. "Please stand by gentlemen."

Both Matten and Barry were watching something no their hologram when the gate opened ever so slightly and a young woman walked out. She looked very confident and had some sort of a writing pad in her hand. She was wearing a white shirt and a black skirt that stretched up to her knees. She was also wearing a black blazer that went up to her hips.

She walked up to Matten and Barry. "Good morning gentlemen. My name is Alexia Grena. I got a notification from the robot saying that you guys wanted to meet me. What is the matter, gentlemen?" asked Alexia.

"We are from the Alpha Crime Hunt team. My name is Barry and this is my colleague Matten. We have to show you guys something very important", said

Barry. "We have something that involves your new device called Elemeasure."

Alexia took a good look at the ID cards which Matten and Barry had opened on their holograms. "Please follow me inside", said Alexia as she started to walk into the building.

The headquarters was huge. There was one big building in the middle of it all with a giant NASA logo on it. All three of them were heading to that center building. Alexia pulled out her hologram and called someone and talked on the hologram for about 40 seconds. Then she turned to Matten and Barry and started to speak to them. "Since you guys are from Alpha, you guys can even talk to the administrator of NASA. Would you guys like to talk to him?" she asked. "We would like to talk to anyone who can help us with the Elemeasure", replied Matten.

"Very well, follow me gentlemen", said Alexia as she walked towards the nearby elevator. The elevator automatically started moving. After about half a minute, the elevator stopped. They go out and walked along a long corridor. Matten had seen an uncountable number of robots on his way to this corridor while he had seen only about 30 people. They got to the end of the corridor and there was a door at the end. The door opened automatically and they entered the room.

The room was another world for Matten and

Barry. The room was full of supercomputers and many more highly complicated looking things that they did not even know what they were. There were about 50 people white laboratory coats with the NASA logo stitched onto the coat.

They hovered (on a hoverboard) over to a young and energetic man in one corner of the room. He looked up and was a little confused.

"Can we please borrow you outside for a second?" said Alexia to the man. "Sure", he said. Then all four of them hovered back to the corridor that they had just come from. They hovered back up the corridor. When they were almost at the lift, they turned right where there was a door leading into another room. The word 'ADMINISTRATOR' was written on the door. They went inside the room. The room was large but empty. There were a large levitating glass table and a chair to one corner of the room. There was a serious- looking man sitting on the chair. Matten guessed he was the administrator of NASA. HE was wearing a neatly ironed back suit with a white shirt and a gold-colored tie. He stood up when they came in.

"Good morning gentlemen", he said. "My name is Raymond Eddieworn. I am the administrator of the National Aeronautics and Space Administration. Alexia just told me that you guys are from Alpha. What is the matter? I also was told that you guys have something that is related to the Elemeasure."

"Good morning sir, my name is Matten and this is my colleague Barry. We have something very important that we want you all to see", said Matten and reached for his bag. He took out a file and opened it up. He pulled out the sheets that were in the file. Barry recognized these sheets as the sheets that Matten's grandfather had left in his basement. Matten glanced slightly at the sheets and have them to Raymond.

Raymond received the papers but Matten could see he was a little confused. Raymond was about to read when he spoke. "Shall we sit down?" he asked. "Sure", replied Matten. Raymond went over to his table and pressed a button. As soon as he pressed the button, a seven- seater rounded couch rose out of the floor next to the table. All of them went over and sat on the couch. Then, Raymond started to read the sheets aloud.

He took a few minutes to read the sheets at the end of it everyone was shaken. No one could believe such as thing could even exist. Everyone was now deadly serious.

"And where is the block of Clantonium?" asked Raymond in a deep, dark voice. "In this bag", replied Matten pointing at the backpack that he carried. "Can we see it?" Raymond asked. "Yes but extreme precautions must be taken", said Matten. "First of all we must all wear high-quality breathing masks and no one can touch it even by mistake."

That was when Alexia did something on her hologram and a few seconds later, a robot carrying 5 breathing masks on a tray came into the room. Everyone in the room picked up one each and put them on. Then the robot left. There was a moment of absolute silence. Then Matten reached for the bag and picked it up. He slowly unzipped it. There was a large metal container and he pulled it out. He took the lid off and there it was covered in an extremely thick blanket. There were a pair of thick rubber gloves and Matten put them on. Then he picked it up and slowly took the blanket off. And then, there it was. All three of the NASA members could not believe what they were seeing.

"I....I....I cannot believe what I am seeing," said Raymond. "This is crazy!"

Alexia and the other man were just too shocked to speak.

"Now, this is why I got this over here. I thought testing this with the new device that you guys have made called Elemeasure will be useful to determine the overall danger levels associated with Clantonium", said Matten.

"Sure, let's get the test done immediately", said Raymond as he was getting up. His eyes were still fixed on the block of Clantonium.

Everyone got up. All of them stepped onto their hoverboards and went over to the door and outside. They took the lift and went a few stories down. The door opened. All of this happened automatically. Then they went into a room at the end of the corridor.

This room was also very big. There were a couple of robots carrying a few different things. But there was something big in the center of the room and it was covered with a thin cloth. Matten had an intuition that it was the Elemeasure. They went over to it and got off their hoverboards.

"This is the Elemeasure", said the man who was wearing a lab coat. "By the way, my name is Ronald Henry. I am the designer of the Elemeasure. I also am the head of the research team here at NASA", he said.

He leaned over and removed the cloth that was covering it revealing a white, almost cube-shaped machine that was almost the same size as a quadbike. There was a large display to the left of the machine and Ronald went over to the screen and made some preparations. He took about five minutes to complete the preparations and then he put on the rubber gloves that Matten was wearing. Then he picked the block of Clantonium up. He then walked to the right of the machine where there was a pretty large door. Ronald pulled the door up and placed the block inside. Then he removed the gloves and went back to the screen.

Everyone else was watching him silently. Then he made some final touches on the screen and finally a large green button appeared on the screen that read 'BEGIN TEST'. Ronald turned back to look at the remaining members. All of them nodded simultaneously for acknowledgment. Then Ronald took a deep breath and touched that button. There was a timer that appeared on the screen that was counting down from six minutes. All five of them were waiting patiently for the timer to run out. After six long minutes, the time finally ran out.

Ronald walked forward to something that looked like a peephole next to the screen. Ronald had to look into the peephole to know the result.

The machine was intentionally designed that way. Ronald leaned and looked into the peephole. As soon as he looked in, he was thrown back. Whatever the result was, it had shaken him.

"What is it?" asked Raymond. Ronald did not respond. "Ronald, what is it?" Raymond asked again but this time in a much louder voice.

Ronald finally gathered the courage to speak. "It's…….it's……..16.51", he said in a trembling voice. Barry gasped. Everyone else was speechless. This new element was more than two times more dangerous than Plutonium.

They had all gone back to Raymond's room and were seated on the couch. They were all sitting there just collecting their thoughts.
Raymond broke the silence. "This thing has the capacity to destroy this whole headquarter. This thing is extremely dangerous. Thank goodness there's only a small piece of this thing", he said. That was when Matten turned to him. Raymond had a bad feeling that he knew what Matten was going to say.

Raymond spoke again.

 "Oh no, please do not tell me.....

...there's more", Matten finished the sentence. "There is much, much more."

CHAPTER 4: THE INVESTIGATION

They were all sitting there quietly when Ronald broke the silence.

"I think I can do some research on this and understand more", he said. "You guys can leave the block of Clantonium so I can do some research upon it. I can find out how it can affect our planet and also find outs sort of antidote for it if I may say so."

"Sure, but please take extreme precautions before even thinking about it", said Matten. Then Matten and Barry got up. They headed to the door and left. They went down in the lift and did not speak to each other in the lift. They hovered all the way to the main gate and went over to the car. From there they got back to New York the same day itself. They stayed at Barry's place.

Barry's house was quite big for just one person. Even though there was only one person living, there were several robots that included two humanoid robots and several other robots that were used for chores around the house. Unlike Matten, Barry was all into technology. He would be the first one to go out and get the latest tech that release.

Barry's house had five bedrooms and his living room was massive. He had a completely automated kitchen that would prepare his food and also do all the dishes.

Barry welcomed Matten into his house and offered him a room on the third story as that room had the least amount of automation in it.
Although the room had virtual assistants that can turn on and off lights and draw the curtains, the room had no robots moving around the room and that gave Matten some peace of mind.
Matten's luggage was already at Barry's house and was placed in the living room. One of the humanoid robots carried the luggage to Matten's room. Matten was exhausted when he got to his room and sat down. He had a really long day and it was almost 10 pm. He went into the bathroom and took a quick shower. Then he went down for dinner. The food was ready and Barry was waiting for him at the dining table.

Matten guessed that the main course was prepared by the robots but Barry had also bought some expensive vine.

Then they started eating. Matten really liked the

food for once. He ate really fast, he was very hungry.

Then he went to bed. The next morning he woke up at 6 am. He got dressed and went down for breakfast. After breakfast, they went to work in the same car that Alpha had provided. They did some paperwork the whole day at the Alpha headquarters.

Then they went back and went on with their routine like normal.

They kept going on with their usual routine when one day when Matten was about to leave from work, he got a call from NASA. He knew that it was something that involved Clantonium. He attended the call. A 3D figure of Ronald came upon the hologram.

"Matten, I want you to come to the NASA headquarters immediately", he said.

"Sure", Matten said and hung up. He got into his car and drove off. One the way he also messaged Barry to come to the NASA headquarters.

He reached the headquarters in about five minutes. He ran up to the room where the Elemeasure was placed. Barry was already there. Everyone had a very serious face. Every one that Matten knew in the NASA headquarters was there; Ronald, Raymond, and Alexia. They were all sitting down on a couch in the room. Matten walked over and joined them. Ronald started to speak.

"I did a lot of research in the past month and the news you are about to here is not good news at all", he said in a low and dark voice. It was extremely quiet. "We went to the location that you went to Cairo with the geographical team. They did some experiments in the Clantonium ore and came to a conclusion. Clantonium, from deep within the Earth, has been slowly coming towards the crust from the beginning of the planet. It just kept coming out and now it is dangerously close to the crust. If it comes out, it will wipe out the entire planet. And by wipeout I mean kill everything alive; the biggest animals all the way to smallest microbes and everything in between. And the worst news is that we have not much time before Clantonium pushes its way out of the Earth's crust."

"How much time's left?" Matten asked.

"That is the worst news of all", said Ronald. "We have just 9 months before it comes out of the crust."

Everyone fell silent. Everyone was thinking about death, except Ronald. He knew there still was a way around this mess.

CHAPTER 5: THE ONLY WAY

"So we are all going to die", said Matten in the lowest voice he ever could. Matten was kind of realizing that after all, he was scared of death. Everyone was quiet for a long time. Then Ronald spoke,

"No, we are not. The geographical team analyzed the data and listed what it is made up of. It is made up of a completely new substance that we named Merum. That is what causes all the bleeding and also responsible for producing some sort of static electricity automatically. We do not know how it does that but it somehow manages to do that.

Recently our space exploration team has discovered a new planet that they named RD-12. So it so happens that the planet is made of something we named Weton. Weton is the exact opposite of chemical properties when it is compared with Merum. They did some research and officially confirmed that we can use Weton to neutralize Merum. Similar to the way we can neutralize an acid with a base."

"Where is this planet?" Matten asked.

"That is the problem. It is thirty-thousandth of a light-year away", Ronald said.

There was a moment of silence. Everyone was looking at each other. Then Barry spoke. "Can we go there and bring it back?"

"Yes, technically we can", said Ronald. "We at NASA, have been working and a new technology called Blastron that harvests the energy of the sun no matter how far the sun is from the rocket and convert it into radiating heat waves that can boost the rocket at 15 miles per second. If we can travel that fast we can reach RD-12 in exactly three months. But there is a problem. Blastron has never been tested before anywhere. We do not know how it will perform on such a long journey.

And here is the biggest problem; there has to be a good number of people on the rocket going in the rocket because landing that far away from Earth is going to be difficult. The rocket will have to go through a path of dust to reach the other side. But that dust has the potential to interfere with our signals so there is a chance to lose contact with the rocket. So to handle the landing, we need someone with flight experience onboard." Then he told something that shocked everyone. "And we do not know if the rocket will make it back. In addition to that, we have a lot of payloads and the calculations might vary according to the amount of the substance that the mining team on board might collect.”

“If we all understand the complications and the risks involved are if we are still willing to go ahead, we can start construction today”, said Raymond. “It will take about three months to construct the rocket with today's sophisticated technology. A few decades ago, this would have been impossible but with today’s technology, it might very well be. So do we want to proceed?”

“What other choice do we have? We rather risk a few lives and save the whole world or die with the rest of it with the guilt internally killing all of us”, said Matten.

“Very well, we will have to take a few permissions and there will be a lot of paperwork to do. But I must say, this has to be completely confidential”, said Raymond.

Barry had been silent the whole time. For him, he wished he had never known what he just got to know in the past few minutes.

Both Matten and Barry returned home. They had not talked about this at all. It was dinner time and both of them were sitting at the dining table. There were grilled cheese and tomato soup for dinner. They had just begun to eat when Barry spoke. “A few months ago I met a guy called Tazen Gutler. He is well educated in aeronautical science and seems to be a nice guy. There was one noteworthy though. Even though he was very well educated, he does not work anywhere. I asked him why and he said that his dream was to make some new technology that will change the world. He seems to be a really nice guy and I think he will be willing to help with our problem now."

"Ok sure. We'll tell NASA to talk to him tomorrow", said Matten. Then they finished their dinner and went to bed.

The next morning both of them went over to the NASA headquarters. They went inside and behind the main building were the construction site and the building. As soon as they got to the construction site, their jaws were dropping. They had never seen so much technology in one place. There were a massive number of robots working on multiple different things at the same time. Matten saw someone and recognized him. It was Ronald. He walked up to Matten and Barry. "What do you think about our progress?" he asked. He sounded very energetic and almost happy. "Man I feel like I am hallucinating", said Barry. Matten noticed a huge shed next to the construction site. "What's in there?" he asked Ronald. "Oh, that is where the engine is being manufactured.
The Blastron boosters are being installed", he said. "Oh, ok", said Matten. Then they wished him good luck and they left for work.

Matten's and Barry's routine was as normal and they were approaching the end of the construction. The three months that NASA told the construction would take was over. It was the day that NASA told the construction would be over. Matten and Barry had not visited the NASA headquarters in the past month and they had no idea how the final result would look.

They got ready early in the morning and headed to the headquarters. They reached the headquarters in no time and went in. They went into the construction site and there it was. It stood there big and bold. It looked just like a space shuttle from 2020 and Matten actually liked the retro look. But there was one major difference. This shuttle was much, much bigger than the usual size. Barry guessed it was at least 3 times bigger. That was when Raymond walked up to him. He was wearing a black suit and a dark red tie with a light gold shirt. Alexia was next to him. He shook hands with Matten and Barry and guided them to the office. There he explained the plan.

"So we went with the space shuttle skeleton as that design is really convenient to install the Blastron boosters. We have a total of 5 boosters and no boosters for landing as RD-12 has a really hard and flat surface on which the space shuttle can land like a normal airplane. The shuttle has enough space to accommodate 40 crew members on board and can comfortably fly though the dust without any physical damage on the shuttle. There is also enough space for each crew member to comfortably live for six months. There is one thing that all crew members have to do though; all the crew members on board have to exercise for at least 3 hours a day to prevent muscle loss. Muscle losses will definitely happen if the crew doesn't exercise as there is no gravity on the shuttle. We did not have enough time to take a shuttle that can make its own gravity. We could have achieved gravity if we constructed a rotating torus but that would take an estimated time of 6 months to construct. 29 members of NASA are ready for the journey."

"So that included me and Barry right?" asked Matten.

"No. We can only send people who have previous flight experience. And there will be a lot for different forces acting on the human body. In addition to that a lot of tests have to be taken before a human can fly", said Raymond.

"What! No way. I and Barry will fly", said Matten.

"Matten, please understand. It is not possible", said Raymond.

"Well if you have to take any tests, take them now. And do not worry about the forces. If we do not make this a successful trip, we will not be alive anyway", said Barry.

Raymond thought for a minute. Then he slightly nodded his head. "So, when are we flying?" asked Matten.

"Tomorrow", said Raymond. Then he reached underneath his table and picked up something that looked like a chart and it was rolled into a roll. "This is the space shuttle printed out on this chart. You can take this home. I will send other specs to you hologram", he said.

Matten opened it up. The chart was very big and the image looked beautiful. Matten and Barry looked at the chart for some time and then he rolled it back up. Matten and Barry decided to go back home. They were supposed to come back for the test at noon. On the way back, Barry had an idea. "Should we call Tazen Gutler along for the trip? He, after all, is in the same field like this and is pretty good at this", said Barry.

Matten thought for a minute. Then he spoke. "Yeah sure, we'll ask NASA for their opinion. If they agree we can have him with us. But I'm not sure he's going to agree. This is such a dangerous mission."

"Yeah, I know. But we'll just ask him", said Barry.

It was noon and they were back at the NASA headquarters. They were taken to a lab in the headquarters and they were shot with 4 syringes each. Tazen agreed to join them. The whole situation was explained to him and he was willing to take the risk. All three of them were put through extreme and vigorous testing and finally, they were approved for the flight. The whole launch was planned and was supposed to be executed in secrecy. If the public knew about this, there would be a lot of commotion and anxiety. So the whole thing was very confidential and was known to the people of NASA only.

After the entire test, they were sent to the resting quarters in the NASA headquarters itself. They were not allowed to go home as they had to be in observation for at least six hours. They were given comfortable places to stay and the rest of the crew was also getting ready. That night at dinner, Matten, Barry, and Tazen were introduced to the other crew members. They spoke for a while and were ready for bed. He launch was supposed to take place at 8 am the next morning. All the crew members go a good night's rest and were awake at 5:30 am the next morning. They all gathered at the preparation center where they would be given a little bit of briefing and last minute medications. Everyone gathered around the center and took their seats. Ronald was giving the briefing. He walked over in front of them and started to speak. "Good morning respected space explorers. Today all of you will embark on a mission bigger than anything known to mankind. In fact, your mission's success is going to determine the future existence of mankind itself. You will be a part of mission Qtron 2080 for the next 6 months." Qtron 2080 was the name given to this mission. "For food, there are two steps taken for preparing the food which is more than sufficient for everyone on board for over 12 months. We have used dehydration and molecular shrinking. Let us use a hamburger for example. First, all the water is removed from this hamburger. Then it is placed in a machine that was recently designed by NASA.

What this machine does is shrink each molecule of the burger to one-hundredth of the original size. Then this shrunk burger is coated with a powder that keeps it from rotting. All this processed food is stored in the lower deck of the shuttle. All you guys have to do is pick up the meal you want to eat and place it in the machine that almost looks like an OTG. What this machine does is expands the molecules to original size and also adds back the moisture that was removed from the food in the first place. The water situation in the shuttle is quite simple and all of you already know it but please allow me to recap. There is a fixed volume of water that is already circulating throughout the shuttle. As this water is being used up, it will also be secreted. The water from the secretions will be collected and purified to a great extent that the purified water is as fresh as pure water. Then the secretions will be disposed of out into space.

There are also three massive tanks of water just in case there was a loss of water. The situation with the air is quite similar. The used air will be purified and will be fit for consumption again. Just like water, there are three massive tanks of liquefied oxygen just in case.

As you all know the whole flight, if it goes according to plan, will be completely automated. But as all of you know, the shuttle will have to fly thought a patch of dust that might interfere with the signal. If it does then you guys will have to manually take over. The flight team had trained for this so there is no need to worry even if the signal gets cut. If in case it does not get cut, the flight will continue to be automated for the whole journey. After the shuttle lands there, the mining team will take care of the whole mining process. Then again if there is no signal problem, the take-off will be automated, if not there will be manual take off. And one last thing, all of you are given a workout schedule and you must follow it to prevent muscle loss. And last but not least, I hate to say it but enjoy your flight. Any questions?" asked Barry. No one replied. Everyone was clear with the plan and very nervous. None of them had informed their family about this and they had just said that they had some long term project that would take about six months.

All the last-minute tests were done and medication was given. All of the crew members headed to the shuttle that was all ready to take off. It was already at the launch pad and was attached to a rocket. The rocket would boost the shuttle outside Earth's atmosphere and from there it would detach and fly on its own using NASA's new Blastron technology.

The crew members were in the shuttle and the countdown began. 10…9…8…7…6…5…4…3…2…1 and ignition and lift off.

They were on their way on the journey. At first, the whole thing was vibrating like crazy but as soon as they exited Earth's atmosphere and when they were detached from the rocket, the whole thing was so smooth that they did not even feel like they were moving.

After about 3 minutes after the shuttle got detached from the rocket, the radio started to buzz and suddenly they could hear Raymond speaking. "Congratulations Qtron 2080 for making it the cruise stage of the flight. Now the only next challenging part for the crew members of Qtron 2080 is after two months when the shuttle will approach the patch of dust."

CHAPTER 6: THE PATCH
OF DUST AND MINING

The whole journey had been very smooth so far. There were no major problems. After about a month into the journey, there was a failure in one of the Blastron boosters but that issue was immediately fixed by the ground crew members. The routine of the crew members was quite simple; they would wake up, got to the toilet, brush their teeth, eat breakfast, exercise for three hours and just hang around for the rest of the day and go to bed. But today is going to be a heart-stopping day for the crew members. It was two months since the launch and it was the day that Qtron 2080 would pass through the patch of dust. They were scheduled to pass the dust patch in 10 more minutes. The flight crew members were ready at the controls of the shuttle in case the signal was lost. Everyone had taken their positions around the radio controls to somehow keep the connection going. And in no time, they were at the patch of dust. "Ok Qtron 2080, we are at the patch of dust. Please turn your radio off and turn it on once we reach the other end of the patch", said the voice on the radio. "The technician on board said as he was told turned the radio off. And they were in the patch of dust. The sound on the shuttle sounded like raindrops falling on a car. The whole journey through the dust lasted 95 seconds and they were out of the dust patch.

The technician immediately turned on the radio. There was some glitching noise and it continued for a long time. Everyone held their breath. There was absolute silence for a few seconds. And then, miraculously, the radio started to speak. "Congratulations Qtron 2080 on passing the dust patch. All systems are in working condition and automated flying will continue", it said.

Everyone aboard the shuttle was thrilled. Whatever they feared did not happen. The patch of dust was not dense enough to interfere with the signal. So that meant that the entire journey now would be automated.

Everyone soon got back to their normal routine. Another month passed in it was now time to land. Five minutes before landing, everyone took their positions and soon the wheels were deployed and then, for the first time ever the wheels touched a solid surface. They had landed! After touchdown, the shuttle took about two and a half minutes to completely come to a halt. After 10 minutes after the shuttle stopped, everyone was ready in their spacesuits. Then came the magical moment everyone had been waiting for. The door of the shuttle opened. The planet was very smooth and plain. The planet also had an orange-colored glow to it.

Everyone stepped out of the aircraft one by one. The mining team got to work immediately. The rear trapdoor was open and after the drilling team drilled the planet and created small boulders of Weton, the loading team loaded it onto the shuttle. While the mining team was doing their work, all other crew members were roaming the planet. Everyone was supposed to report back at the shuttle in two hours because the mining team would be done by that time.

Two hours were up and the mining team was done with their work. Everybody was back at the shuttle and everybody got one good look at RD-12 before the door was closed and sealed. The place where the huge amounts of Weton were stored had spinning blades that would chop up the boulders of Weton and over the course of the next three months before the shuttle returns, the boulders would become a fine powder.

They were back on their way. Everyone was confident that the world would be saved. No one knew a new problem would arise soon.

CHAPTER 7: THE BETRAYAL

Their journey back was as effortless as the journey to RD-12. The routine of everyone was normal. Matten had so far been enjoying the flight. Now that he knew that the world could be saved, he had some peace of mind. Matten had just finished eating lunch and he was floating towards the entertainment section where there were some magnetic chess boards and some more board games. Matten went inside and saw that Tazen was sitting there just lost in thoughts.

"Hey Tazen, do you want to play some chess?" asked Matten. "Sure", he replied. Matten started arranging the chessboard while Tazen slowly drifted to the hatch of the entertainment area and closed it and locked it. Matten thought that was weird but he thought Tazen was doing that to just avoid the noise coming from the rest of the people chatting outside. Matten was almost done arranging the chessboard when he heard a click that sounded very familiar to him. Matten knew what that click was.

That click was the sound of a pistol reloading.

Matten turned his head to Tazen and saw that he was pointing a pistol straight to his head. Tazen started to speak.

"I can't believe you just let me come along on this trip without checking my identity. Let me tell you a little story. Long, long ago in 2019-20, your grandfather's company was the most successful space research organization on the Earth. Your grandfather and his boss Brandon Lync were so successful in this field that they crushed all other private space research organizations including my grandfather's company. And if your grandfather and his stupid boss were not that successful, my grandfather's company would have also become successful, I could have been filthy rich by now. And on top of that success, your grandfather's boss was planning a project called JETLAX 4000 that would make the company unbelievably rich. He had invested his whole company's worth into that project. That was a golden opportunity for my grandfather. He attached a self-destructing microphone to your grandfather's shoe and overheard the whole plan. There was something called the HASRET without which the whole rocket would be a failure. Well, the only sensible thing to do at that time was to destroy the HASRET. And that was what he did. Brandon Lync had a bunch of security features that included his body parts so my grandfather killed him and used his body parts to unlock a vault in which he HASRET was stored. That way his revenge on Brandon Lync was over. And you might have heard that your grandfather's parent's plane exploded and they died. Well, all engines exploded simultaneously on the aircraft and do you know how that happened? My grandfather shot four sticky bombs onto the engines of the aircraft after it took it and blasted them.

Sure it did kill a few extra people but it did get the job done. And I am also in the story. Do you remember how your parents died in a car crash? Well, I was the one who arranged the crash. By now you probably guessed who I am. My real name is not Tazen Gutler. My real name is Tazen Ruder. And that brings me to the ultimate reason why I'm going to kill you now. Because of your grandfather, my grandfather could not become rich and that directly affect me now because now I'm not rich. My grandfather left me a note telling me to completely get rid of the Hensworth race and that would be achieved as soon as this bullet lands inside your brain."

Matten was speechless. There was a flow of emotions through his heart. He felt a lot of anger at the same time he was crying. But Tazen did not notice one thing. As he was speaking Matten slowly kept moving back up to a point where he reached the back wall. Tazen was almost touching the hatch of the entertainment area. Matten pressed a button on the wall and the hatch flung open. The hatch sent him flying and coincidently Barry was right outside so he came in and locked the hatch. "What happened in here?" asked Barry. Matten told him everything. When Matten was done, Tazen was back to normal but his gun was in Matten's hands. Matten was about to shoot Tazen when he heard another gun click. He turned around only to see Barry pointing a gun straight at Matten's head. Matten was extremely shocked. He could not believe his eyes. The man who he had trusted with his life had just betrayed him. "I'm sorry Matten", he said. Matten was so frozen that he let go of his gun and could not grab it back even though it was right in front of him. "Tazen agreed to offer me money for this and at the end of the day, only money matters." Barry floated over to Tazen. Barry was about to shoot Matten when Tazen said he wanted to shoot him and Barry gave the gun to him. Tazen received the gun an instantaneously shot Barry in the head. Matten was surprised. Matten then quickly reached for his gun and slipped it into his back pocket while Tazen was busy getting away from the big droplets of blood.

Then he pointed the gun towards Matten. "Once I kill you, there is no way I can get away alive on Earth. So, once I kill you, I will kill everyone on board with the sub-machine guns that I have in the back of the shuttle and manually change the path of the shuttle so that it crashes into a big celestial body and the shuttle will get destroyed. Why will I do this you might ask and the answer is pretty simple; why should anyone be alive if I am not? So Mr. Matten, any last words?" he asked. Matten knew he cannot afford to die. He dying now will leave the faith of humanity in the hands of a madman. Matten had to somehow escape. "Yes", replied Matten to Tazen's question. "Watch out for that blob of blood", said Matten. Tazen did exactly as Matten had anticipated. He took his eyes off Matten for a second and Matten did not miss that opportunity. He pulled out the gun from his back pocket and shot just one and the bullet stopped only inside Tazen's head. Tazen was dead. Matten took a deep breath and sighed. He took about 10 minutes to collect his thoughts. Then he went out and explained what had just happened to the crew members and also told it to the ground crew members. The rest of the days on the flight were still normal for everyone else except for Matten. He felt betrayed.

Then finally it was the day that they return to Earth. The landed on a runway that NASA had constructed and everyone got out. A medical check was done on everyone and everyone was absolutely fine. A team at NASA took in charge of spreading the Weton powder all over the world. Research had confirmed this will have no bad on marine life and on any other life form on the Earth so the plan was to spread this powder from the sky onto the whole surface area of the Earth. Weton was much stronger than Merum that was present in Clantonium.

The following day, everything went according to plan and the planet was safe. All the Clantonium had been neutralized.

CHAPTER 8: A FEW YEARS LATER

It was now many years later and Matten had changed. He totally forgot about the betrayal. He had a wife named Eria Hensworth and two twin boys who he named Dwane and Brane Hensworth. After a long time, Matten finally had people to call family.

About the author:

Born in December 2004, I wrote this mini novel, I was in the 9th grade and was 15 years old. As a person who was always interested in writing, I finally put my foot down and wrote my first book. Hope you enjoyed the book!

THANK YOU FOR READING!